D0752855

The Christmas Wish

The Christmas Wish

Richard M. Siddoway

Bookcraft
Salt Lake City, Utah

Copyright © 1996 by Richard M. Siddoway

All rights reserved. No part of this book may be reproduced
in any form or by any means without permission in writing
from the publisher, Bookcraft, Inc., 1848 West 2300 South,
Salt Lake City, Utah 84119.

Bookcraft is a registered trademark of Bookcraft, Inc.

Library of Congress Catalog Card Number: 96–86341
ISBN 1–57008–295–2

Second Printing, 1996

Printed in the United States of America

Chapter One

Thanksgiving dinner never changed. It was an anchor in a sea of turmoil. The heavy oak table my grandfather brought from England was covered with a thick linen tablecloth to hold the feast that had been prepared for us. Only on this occasion did my grandmother set the table with the Spode china emblazoned with the family crest.

My job was to polish the two silver candelabra which bore the three long, flickering tapers, placed near the center of the table. The menu never varied: mashed potatoes, gravy, peas, cranberry jelly, and stuffing surrounded the golden roast turkey. We knew that pumpkin pie was waiting in the kitchen.

Although Thanksgiving dinner never changed, there were changes in our family. One Independence Day, my grandparents had attended our town's traditional early morning breakfast and flag ceremony at the city park. They had brought folding lawn chairs to sit on, and as my grandfather stood to honor the flag, he suffered a heart attack. Following the pledge of allegiance, he slumped to the ground; and by the time the ambulance delivered him to the hospital, he was gone.

I felt a special loss because my grandparents had raised me since I was a boy of four. My father and mother were both killed in an automobile accident when a driver fell asleep at the wheel and crossed over the center line to collide head-on with my parents' car. My grandparents buried their only son and daughter-in-law and brought me home to live with them.

For the next twenty years they filled my need for parents, and perhaps I filled their need for a child. It was my grandmother who took me to school the first day. It was her refrigerator door that displayed my treasured artwork. It was she to whom I returned each day from school.

My grandfather let me work beside him in his garden. It was at his side that I learned to tell weeds from flowers . . . most of the time. It was he who stood beside me when I opened my first savings account.

In high school I enjoyed some modest success as a basketball player. My grandparents were always there, always in the same spot—four rows up in the bleachers behind our team. Although I never threw in the winning basket in the final moments, Grandpa was quick to point out that the point or two I contributed during the game helped put us in a position where it was possible to win.

I went to work at my grandfather's insurance agency when I was eighteen. My grandparents offered both encouragement and financial help to get me through college, even when I changed my major and dragged on an extra year. A picture of me in my cap and gown graced the top of the piano in their living room.

The following year I brought Carol Ann home to introduce her to them. As time progressed, Grandpa presided at the wedding breakfast and helped us with a down payment for our house. We often visited their home for Sunday dinner.

And so we were there for Thanksgiving dinner, the three of us—Grandma, Carol Ann, and me. "William, dear, would you please bless the food?" asked my grandmother. I nodded and we bowed our heads. I offered thanks for the food and asked for a blessing on my grandmother at this holiday time of year. There was a mixed air of celebration and melancholy as we ate our Thanksgiving meal.

"Grandma Nell," I said after we had somehow found room for a piece of pie, "I know how Grandpa simply refused to talk about Christmas until after Thanksgiving, but since we've had dinner, Carol Ann and I were wondering something."

"What's that?"

"Well, we'd like to get you something for Christmas that you'd really like."

"Oh, my dear," she replied, "when you've lived as long as I have, there isn't much to wish for. You just save your money. I don't need anything."

"But," I protested, "there must be something you'd like. Something you've always wanted. We . . . we insist."

I focused on my grandmother sitting at the other end of the table. No strand of her silver-white hair was out of place. Although she was seventy-five years old, she looked at least ten years, perhaps fifteen years younger. In the candlelight she displayed the same loveliness that had captivated my grandfather for over fifty years.

I watched a small frown crease her face. "There is one

thing," she said in a voice barely above a whisper. "Oh dear, it's a foolish thing. I'm embarrassed to even bring it up."

"What is it?" asked Carol Ann.

"Oh, nothing," she replied. I noticed a blush had risen in her cheeks. "I shouldn't even think about it."

"Please tell us," persisted my wife.

My grandmother struggled for a moment, then rose from her chair. "Just a minute," she said as she left the dining room and walked down the hallway toward her bedroom. In a moment she returned with a small, black, leather-bound book in her hand. She seated herself and held the volume in front of her. "This is your grandfather's journal—actually it's only one of almost three dozen books. He wrote nearly every night of our marriage."

"And you?" I queried.

"Oh, I have my journals too. We had an agreement. Because we wanted to be able to write anything, no matter how personal, these books were strictly off-limits. I never violated that agreement until Will died." She looked down at the tabletop and I saw the beginnings of tears in her eyes. "Oh, this is silly!" she said.

"Please, Grandma," I said.

"What does this have to do with Christmas?" asked Carol Ann.

My grandmother opened the journal to a page she had marked with a slip of paper. "William," she said, handing me the open book, "just look at this passage."

I took the book from her hands and looked at the spot she indicated. My grandfather had written, "*Mother and I had a disagreement when I arrived home from work. I spent the evening with Lillian."*

I looked into my grandmother's clear blue eyes and saw the tears and the embarrassment. I raised my eyebrows. "Who is Lillian?"

She shook her head gently. "I have no idea. If you really want to get me a Christmas present, that's what I want. I want you to find Lillian."

Chapter Two

"May I take the journal?" I asked my grandmother. "It may help us. It may give some clue."

Grandma nodded her head. "There are no other clues, but take it. Take all of them if you think it will help." She was striving to regain her composure. "We were married fifty-two years, you know, and I never had one moment when I doubted Will's love and commitment. I know this is foolish, but ever since I read that passage I haven't been able to stop wondering who this woman is and why Will ran to her."

"Now, Grandma," I said, "you don't know anything about this—"

"I know, and that's what is bothering me. Not knowing."

At the end of the evening my wife and I took a half-dozen of my grandfather's journals and left for home. "Where are we going to look?" asked my wife.

"I have no idea," I admitted. "Maybe we'll find some help in these journals. Lillian. Just Lillian, no last name, no hint of who she is."

"William, is it possible, just possible that your grandfather had a . . . a . . ." My wife struggled for the right word. "A . . . relationship with another woman?"

"Never!" I said emphatically.

"Just wondering," said my wife.

We carried the journals into our home and I arranged them on the mantel above our fireplace. Written on the first page of each small book was the date of the first entry in that volume. Apparently my grandmother had not arranged them in chronological order. The six we brought home had dates spanning nearly three decades. I opened the volume bearing my grandmother's bookmark. The date on the first page was January 1, 1989. I sat down at the kitchen table and began reading through the journal. Many of the entries were not dated. It was clear that my grandfather was in the habit of jotting down just a thought or two each day he made an entry. The "Lillian" entry was not dated but appeared on a page between an entry dealing with an Easter program at church and a comment about needing to fertilize the roses now that they were beginning to bloom. *He visited Lillian in April,* I thought to myself. *Whoever she is.*

I read the volume from beginning to end. There was no other mention of Lillian. I picked one of the other journals from the mantel and read through it. Again, Lillian's name did not appear.

"Are you coming to bed?" called my wife from the bedroom.

I closed the journal and made my way to the room. "There's no other mention of her," I whispered in the dark.

"How odd," replied my wife. "Does it mention anyone else?"

"Yes, a few people, but no mention of Lillian."

"Maybe one of them would know who Lillian is. Maybe that's at least a place to start."

"Maybe."

When I returned home from my office the next afternoon, my wife met me at the door. "I've made a list," she said.

"A list?" I said quizzically. "A list of what?"

"Of all the people in your grandfather's journals. He must have been an awfully private man—other than relatives, there are only ten people with both their first and last names mentioned in those six books. But look, I've found phone numbers or addresses for nine of the ten. They all still live here in town."

I took the list from my wife and looked at the ten names. Eight of them I recognized. They were either neighbors of my grandparents or people with whom my grandfather associated at work.

"I thought about trying to call them and ask about Lillian, but then I thought better of it," said Carol Ann. "Maybe we need to make a personal visit. Who knows, this might be a sensitive issue. I mean, maybe one of these other men . . ." My wife paused. "Oh, you know."

"I understand," I said, "but I just can't believe that my grandfather was involved in any way with another woman." My wife shrugged her shoulders. I brought the list with me to the dinner table and told her what I knew about the names on the list.

"Walter Thomas," I said, looking at the first name. "He owns an insurance agency in town. He and Grandpa were competitors, I guess. I've met him a few times. If anyone on this list would be having an affair, it would be Walter.

"Malachi Foster owns a chain of bakery shops. Cakes, pies, specialty breads, that kind of thing. We buy a lot of sweet rolls from him for refreshment breaks at meetings."

I looked at the third name. "Portia Adams." My forehead wrinkled. "She worked for Grandpa at the bank. She left the bank a long time ago. Grandpa took me with him to visit her once. I really don't know much about her, but at least I can put a face with the name.

"Jorge Castellanas? That's one of the two names that don't ring a bell." I moved on to the next name. "Alicia Cervantes. Golly, I haven't thought about her in years. Her family used to live next door to us. Alicia was a pretty little thing. I haven't seen them in a long time."

"That's the one I can't find a number for," said my wife.

"Which of the journals did you find these names in?" I asked.

"They were scattered through all six of them. Usually they just had the name and a sentence or two that didn't make much sense."

"Like what?"

"Oh, for example, all it said after the next name on the list, Wendel Walker, was something like 'getting better.'"

"Well, Wendel used to work for Grandpa at his insurance agency. He seemed quite a bit older than Grandpa, and I haven't seen him in a long time. I'm surprised he's still alive.

"Amanda Grossbeck," I continued, "that's a name out of the past. She and her sister used to live across the street from us. I think they both lost their husbands in the war. I'm amazed you found a phone number for her." My wife smiled at me.

I turned my attention back to the list. "Maude Carlisle used to keep house for us. I'm not sure why Grandma hired her, but she used to come clean the house and do the washing and ironing. She was kind of a roly-poly woman. I remember she had a rather distinctive odor about her. It wasn't unpleasant, but I don't think I've smelled it since she quit working for us."

When I focused on the next name I had a lurching sensation in my stomach. "Richard LeConte was a disappointment to my grandfather. He worked for Grandpa at the bank and learned everything he could; then when Grandpa needed his support, Richard failed him. I don't have real warm feelings about him."

I looked at the last name and then looked up at the ceiling. "Nope," I said, shaking my head, "I can't place this last name either. Beatrice Yazzie. Sounds like a Navajo name. I just don't remember ever having met her before." I placed the list beside my plate.

"Well," said my wife, "let's hope one of them can give us a lead to Lillian."

"Who knows. After dinner let's see if we can make an appointment for tomorrow night. We might as well start at the top of the list."

Carol Ann busied herself putting dinner on the table.

I leaned back in my chair and thought about my grandfather. What an amazing man. He had started working at the bank when he was barely eighteen years of age. By the time he was thirty he was a vice president, probably because he recognized that people who were arranging mortgages through the bank needed a place to get insurance. So he began an independent insurance agency on the side. The relationship helped the bank as well as the agency.

When the president of the bank retired, the board named Grandpa as president. He had barely turned forty years old. He helped the bank grow from two small offices to a network of thirty-two branches across the state. At the same time, he was president of the insurance agency and was elected to the school board, where he served for twelve years. I had felt both honored and scared silly when he decided to retire and put me in charge of the agency. Thank goodness he was always there to offer advice. Until last July. I felt a lump rising in my throat.

After dinner I picked up the phone and dialed the number by Walter Thomas's name. The phone rang three times and then an answering machine intercepted.

"You have reached the Thomas home. We are unable to come to the phone at the moment. If you will leave your name and number after the beep, we'll get back to you as soon as possible." Beep.

"Mr. Thomas, this is William Martin. I'm wondering if it would be possible to meet with you for a few minutes to discuss . . ." My mind whirled. How would I tell him about Lillian? After a brief pause I continued, ". . . my grandfather. My number is 555-4385." I hung up the phone and turned to my wife. "Got his answering machine. Maybe I should try the next name, but I need to think for a minute how to explain why I want to talk to these people. I mean, it doesn't seem quite right to just come out and ask them if they know anyone named Lillian. Boy, no wonder Grandma wanted someone else to handle this."

The phone rang and I picked up the receiver. "Hello."

"This is Walter Thomas returning your call. What exactly do you want to discuss about your grandfather?" His voice was brusque.

What do I say? I wondered. "Is it possible to meet with you in person?"

"I'm awfully busy," he snapped. "How long do you think this will take?"

"Just a few minutes. I could meet with you any day after four-thirty. I guess you are open on Saturday."

"Oh, all right. Drop by my office tomorrow. I'll expect you at four-thirty. I can give you no more than fifteen minutes." Without waiting for a reply, he hung up the phone.

"Well," I said, turning to Carol Ann, "I have an appointment tomorrow afternoon. Help me figure out what to say so I don't raise more questions than I get answered."

"Honey," my wife said, "if you have as much faith in your grandfather as you seem to have, I'm sure you'll find a way to bring up Lillian without suggesting anything to Mr. Thomas. Do you want me to come with you?"

I thought how rude Walter Thomas had seemed on the phone. "Thanks, but I think I'll handle this one by myself. Who knows, maybe I'll solve the mystery on this first visit."

I folded the list and placed it on the shelf next to our telephone. Three hours later as I climbed into bed, I still didn't know exactly what I was going to say to Walter Thomas. One part of my brain hoped he could answer the question; the other side was afraid that he might know personally and intimately who Lillian was.

Chapter Three

Ten minutes before my appointment with Walter Thomas, I stepped out the front door of our insurance agency into an angry wind. I pulled my overcoat more tightly around me and began the five-minute walk to the Thomas Building. A few leaves danced wildly on the skeletal branches of the trees that lined the sidewalk. Those on the ground swirled around my feet and piled up against the building fronts. The clouds boiled overhead.

Streetlights were flickering on and Christmas lights lit the gathering gloom. Two blocks ahead, my destination glowed brightly. The Thomas Building's twenty-five stories made it the tallest structure in town. I quickened my pace as a gust of wind buffeted me and made the garlands of pine strung over the street gyrate in a wild dance.

I tugged on the front door of the building, struggling against the wind; but once I was within the entryway, automatic doors slid open with a sibilant hiss. The foyer of the Thomas Building rose three stories to a vaulted ceiling from which hung a huge crystal chandelier. A twenty-foot-high Christmas tree stood to the left of the doorway, swathed in gold ribbon and crystal ornaments. The front of the building was constructed with vertical panes of glass that afforded a view to passersby. The wall opposite the windows was covered with matched-grain zebra-wood panels divided only by inch-wide gold stripes. The floor was swathed in blood-red plush carpeting. I walked silently across the carpet and approached the receptionist. Behind her in two-foot-high backlighted gold letters was the Thomas Insurance Agency logo.

"I have an appointment with Walter Thomas," I said, smiling. I handed her my business card.

She inspected my card and smiled back at me, revealing a gleaming set of white teeth. "Just one moment, Mr. Martin," she said. She flicked a switch with her perfectly manicured finger and announced into the telephone, "There's a Mr. Martin here to see Mr. Thomas." She paused a moment, then gestured toward one of the snow-white leather sofas at the side of the receptionist console. "Mr. Thomas will be with you in a minute." She smiled again. I thanked her and made my way to the nearest sofa.

Next to the couch was an end table that appeared to be a solid block of glass, and on it was an assortment of magazines. I fingered through them but found nothing that caught my interest. Christmas carols played softly in the background. I gazed at the Christmas tree, still unsure how I was going to bring up the topic of Lillian with Walter Thomas. I leaned back in the supple leather and closed my eyes.

"Mr. Martin," said the receptionist. My eyes flew open. Walter Thomas stood two steps in front of me. I struggled to my feet and extended my hand. He took it reluctantly.

"Thank you for seeing me," I began.

"This way," he said coldly, and indicated a door to the right of the receptionist with a nod of his white-maned head. I followed behind him. Walter Thomas stood at least three inches over six feet. Although he was nearly sixty-five years of age, he exuded an air of lean good health. He was dressed in a midnight blue suit, crisply starched white shirt, and muted maroon paisley tie.

The doorway opened into a paneled hallway lined with offices. Walter Thomas strode confidently to the end of the hallway and opened the door to his office. The room was decorated in shades of turquoise and teal. An enormous impressionistic painting hung behind his glass-topped desk. The office occupied the entire width of the Thomas Building, and both side walls were smoked-glass windows, with a view of the garden area that surrounded the building.

"Sit down," commanded Walter Thomas as he pointed in the direction of a chair by his desk. "As I explained to you last night, I'm quite busy." He checked his wristwatch. "I can give you just fifteen minutes. Now, what is it you wanted to know about your grandfather?" He sat in his high-backed swivel chair and tented his fingers together as he gazed at me.

I cleared my throat. "After my grandfather died rather suddenly, my grandmother asked if I could gather some information for her."

"Information?"

"Well, more like remembrances that his friends and acquaintances have of him."

"I'd hardly consider myself to be a friend," spat Thomas.

"I didn't know there was bad blood between the two of you," I replied.

"He was a fool! Between us we could have owned this town." He grasped the arms of his chair and spun around to look out the windows to his right. Suddenly he sprang from his chair and gestured toward the windows. "Surely he told you of my offer."

I shook my head. "I'm afraid not, Mr. Thomas. He was a very private man."

"Come with me," he commanded, and moved quickly to the door of his office. I followed him to an elevator. Walter Thomas jabbed at the button. "Come on, come on," he growled as we waited for the doors to open. Once inside, he punched the button for the twenty-fifth floor. The high-speed elevator rocketed to the top story of the building. When the doors opened he grabbed me by the arm and led me into the hallway.

The entire twenty-fifth floor was encased in windows that gave a panoramic view of our town. Walter Thomas took me to the windows that looked down on Main Street. "Will Martin wasn't all that wealthy, you know, when I first brought him to this very spot." A protective handrail ran around the room. Walter Thomas leaned heavily on it and gazed out of the windows. "But he was bright and honest to a fault. This idea of his to start an insurance agency to provide mortgage insurance at the bank was brilliant. Of course, before that happened the Thomas Agency was the only agency in town. My grandfather started it and my father followed after him. Now I own it." There was unmistakable pride in his voice.

"When Will started his agency my father told me to

go talk to him to see if I could persuade him to let our agency write the insurance instead of going into competition with us. Your grandfather was ten years older than I, but I thought I could win him over. I brought him here and tried to reason with him." Suddenly he turned and his eyes bored into mine. "Do you know what he told me?" I shook my head. "He said, 'Walter, your rates are too high. You need a little competition to keep you honest.'"

Walter Thomas turned back to his view of the city. "I could see the building boom that was going to hit this town. If we could have tied up all those premiums, we'd have . . . well, we'd have been rich beyond our wildest dreams. I offered to make your grandfather a partner in our agency. He refused. He told me that he was happy where he was."

Walter spread his arms. "I told him that all of this could be his, but he just smiled that infuriating little smile of his and said it was time to go." Once more he glared into my eyes. "I don't know if you can understand what I'm saying."

"But you certainly have done well for yourself," I countered. "I don't see why you dislike my grandfather."

"You don't understand. You're as big a fool as he was. We've leased out more than half of this building. Your grandfather's agency—I guess it's your agency now—does twice the business that ours does. If your grandfather had joined with us, we wouldn't find ourselves wondering how we're going to stay afloat." Suddenly his jaw hardened. "Not that we're in any real trouble, you understand."

I nodded my head. Walter Thomas gazed back over the city. "I'm sorry," he said, "I'm very busy." He gestured toward the elevator.

"May I ask just one question, sir?"

"I suppose," he said, regaining his composure. "What is it?"

"I'm trying to contact as many people as I can who knew my grandfather. I have located all of them except a woman named Lillian. Do you by chance happen to know her and where I might find her?"

"Lillian who?" he asked as his forehead wrinkled.

"I don't know her last name. Lillian is all I know."

He shrugged his shoulders. "Sorry, I'm afraid I can't help you." Again he motioned toward the elevator. I took one last look at the Christmas lights winking up at me from the city below and pushed the button for the elevator. Walter Thomas had not moved. He leaned his forehead against the cold glass of the window. He was still standing there as I stepped into the elevator and the door slid shut.

As I left the Thomas Building, snowflakes were being driven almost sideways by the winter wind. I walked briskly toward our agency. After half a block I looked back at the top floor of the Thomas Building, wondering whether Walter was still standing there in the darkness.

When I arrived home that evening, my wife greeted me at the door. "Any success?" she asked brightly.

"I'm afraid not," I replied. "All I learned tonight was that not everybody loved my grandfather." Over dinner I explained what I'd learned from Walter Thomas.

"Who's next on the list?" asked my wife, undaunted.

"Malachi Foster, the baker. I'd better call him now; I'm sure he goes to bed early. He's probably been at his bakery since early this morning." I picked up the telephone and dialed the number Carol Ann had written on the list.

The phone rang twice before a woman answered. "Hello."

"Hello, is Malachi there, please?"

"Just a minute." I heard the phone being put down. "Sweetheart, it's for you."

A few moments later Malachi Foster picked up the receiver. "Hello, Malachi here."

"This is William Martin, Malachi. I'm trying to gather some information on my grandfather. Is there some time my wife and I could have a few minutes with you?"

"Anytime for Will Martin's grandson, anytime. Just say when."

"Tomorrow's Sunday; would the next evening be convenient? Say about seven?"

"Seven it is," Malachi replied, then after a pause said, "Oh, Monday nights we have to stay a little late at the bakery. Would it be all right if you came there? You know where it is on Maple, don't you?"

"You bet. We'll see you Monday. Thanks, Malachi."

"Good night."

Chapter Four

On Sunday evening we visited my grandmother and told her what progress—or lack of it—we had made on our quest for Lillian. She was not surprised by the reception Walter Thomas had given me. "Will always felt sorry for him, you know. He never felt he got his priorities straight."

"Well, Grandma, I hope that Malachi Foster can help us more than Mr. Thomas did."

"I hope so too, dear," she said as we bade her good night.

The following evening my wife met me at my office as we were closing for the night. We drove to the 300 block on Maple and stopped in front of Foster's Fine Foods. One of the two windows on either side of the entrance displayed a four-tiered wedding cake decorated with dozens of exquisite tiny roses in pale pink. My wife inspected it through the window. "They have a real talent," she said.

The other window showed a gingerbread house nearly three feet high. In front of the gingerbread house, Santa's elves were loading his sled while the jolly old man kissed his wife good-bye at the doorway of the house.

Christmas lights shone brightly around the windows.

We pulled open the door and were immediately enveloped by the odor of freshly baked bread. A dozen or so customers were making their selections from the baked goods that were displayed in glass-fronted cases. Although it was nearly closing time, a few doughnuts, eclairs, and cream puffs enticed us from behind the glass. Malachi Foster stood in the doorway that led to the back of the store. A huge smile was visible underneath his black brush of a mustache. He was a cheerful man, perhaps five and a half feet tall and nearly as wide. He wore an apron that barely covered his ample stomach. He spotted us as we entered his establishment.

"My friends," he called over the hubbub, "please come back here with me." He gestured to a gate at the side of one showcase. Carol Ann and I let ourselves behind the cases and made our way around the clerks who were helping the customers with their choices.

"I am sorry we are in such a mess," he chortled as he enthusiastically shook my hand. Then he pushed me back to arm's length. "You look just like your grandfather. And this beautiful lady must be your bride." He hugged Carol Ann, leaving a smudge of flour on her coat. "Please, please come with me." He turned as quickly as his bulk allowed and led us through the doorway back into the bakery. The room was warm and smelled of dough and baking bread.

A woman who was nearly as large as Malachi quickly came to his side, dusting her hands on her apron. "My wife," Malachi said, smiling. "The joy of my life." She offered her hand to me.

"Sit down, sit down," said Malachi, indicating a table

with four chairs around it. "Ruth, do we have any of that pumpkin pie left?" His wife nodded her head. "Why don't you take a break and the four of us might sample your wares." She smiled and disappeared into a walk-in refrigerator. When she reappeared she had a pie in one hand and a bowl of whipped cream in the other. Malachi rose and retrieved four paper plates and some plastic forks from a nearby shelf.

"Sorry for the paper plates, but we're not very fancy here," he said. His wife quickly cut the pie into pieces, slid a slice onto each of the paper plates, and scooped a generous mound of whipped cream onto each.

"This is the best pumpkin pie I have ever eaten," Carol Ann exclaimed after tasting the first bite.

Malachi and Ruth beamed. "It's an old family recipe," Ruth said. "I'm glad you like it."

At that moment one of the clerks stuck her head around the doorway. "Looks like we're about sold out of everything," she said. "I think I'll start closing up, if you don't mind."

Malachi smiled broadly at her. "Go ahead; turn out the lights and lock the door on your way out. Oh, and if there's anything left that you'd like to take home to your family, please take it. Tell the others to do the same."

The clerk returned the smile and ducked back into the front of the store.

We finished the pumpkin pie in silence and then Malachi pushed his chair back from the table. "What is this that you need to know about your grandfather?" he asked.

I took a deep breath. "Since his untimely death four

months ago, I've been trying to help my grandmother put together sort of a biography of him. I've been talking to some of his old friends and acquaintances . . . just asking them to tell me about my grandfather. Your name appeared in one of his journals, so we thought we might ask you to tell us your feelings about him."

Malachi leaned back in his chair. "Your grandfather was the best friend Ruth and I ever had. He made it possible for us to start our little business."

"How did he do that?" asked my wife.

"We had this idea for a bakery," said Ruth Foster. "There wasn't another one in town, you see. We looked at all the vacant buildings for nearly two years, trying to find one that we could turn into our bakery. At last we found this place."

"It was pretty run-down," continued Malachi. "But we could see that it had potential. We went to the bank to see about getting a loan to buy this building. The bank sent an appraiser out to look at it. I guess he went back and said that he didn't think we could make a go of it. We're kind of off the beaten path, you see."

"But obviously they gave you the money," my wife said, indicating the building around us.

Ruth shook her head. "Not until your grandfather came to our home and talked to us. He listened to us describe our dream and then he went back to the bank and argued our case. A week later he brought us a check for twenty-five thousand dollars."

"Was that what you'd asked for? Was it enough?" I asked.

Malachi and Ruth both nodded their heads. "Ample

for our needs," said Malachi. "We remodeled and opened our bakery three months later. At first we were a little worried that people wouldn't be able to find us, but your grandfather was one of our first customers. Even though it has been over twenty years ago, I can still remember that he ordered three dozen sweet rolls."

"With glaze on them," added Ruth. "They were always his favorite."

"We still serve them at every board meeting," I said.

Malachi smiled broadly. "Word spread and we've enjoyed more success than we ever thought possible. We've opened six other shops since then."

Ruth stood up and went to check the oven. "Nearly done," she announced.

"I'll bet the bank was glad my grandfather convinced them to lend you the money," I said. "And I'll bet it was a great day when you paid off the mortgage and retired that original debt. It reminds me of those old Hollywood movies where the banker delivers the mortgage papers and they are torn up or burned."

"You know," said Malachi, "there were never any mortgage papers that I know of. Your grandfather just delivered the check and we shook hands on it. He dropped by every Friday night on the way home from work and picked up some doughnuts."

"Or sweet rolls," chimed in Ruth.

"I just gave him a payment every month and he wrote me a receipt. One day he told me that the debt was paid in full. He was an honest man and I trusted him."

"Just out of curiosity, what interest rate did you have to pay?" I queried.

"I don't know," said Malachi. "I just trusted your grandfather to treat me fairly. I'm sure he did. But I guess we could figure it out. I have all his receipts in an envelope." He swiveled his chair around to a file cabinet and pulled open a drawer. He retrieved a manila envelope and handed it to me. I opened the clasp and shook the receipts onto the kitchen table. I glanced at several. Each one was for the same amount—five hundred dollars.

My wife started counting the receipts.

"I really appreciate this information about my grandfather," I said. "It has been very interesting." I sucked in my breath. "One of the people he mentions in his diary is a woman named Lillian. Would either of you by chance know anyone by that name?"

Ruth and Malachi looked at each other for a moment; then both shook their heads slowly. "Do you know her last name?" Ruth asked.

"I'm sorry, I don't. It's probably not important."

My wife finished counting the receipts and returned them to the envelope.

Ruth again went to her oven. "They're done, sweetheart," she said, and began removing loaves of bread and placing them on cooling racks.

"Are you getting an early start on tomorrow's baking?" my wife asked with a smile.

"Oh, no," said Ruth, "we come at three o'clock tomorrow morning to do that. These are for the shelter."

I wrinkled my forehead. "The shelter?"

"The homeless shelter," said Malachi. "When we first opened, your grandfather came here Monday nights on

26

the way home from work and bought everything we had left at the end of the day and had us take it to the homeless shelter. After a while we told him that they needed bread more than they needed cream puffs, and we just started baking a few loaves every Monday night." He went to help his wife remove the loaves of bread from the ovens.

"It's not much," said Ruth. "We just try to help a little."

"How many loaves do you bake for them each week?" asked Carol Ann.

"Not very many," smiled Malachi with an embarrassed look on his face. "About a hundred."

"Would you like to go with us while we deliver them?" asked Ruth. "The poor dears seem to like eating it while it's warm." Quickly she and her husband slipped the steaming loaves into paper bags.

"I'm sorry there's not room for you in the delivery van," said Malachi, "but you're welcome to follow us if you'd like."

"Thank you, but unless you need our help, I think we'll head home and try to jot down what you've told us."

Ruth poked her head into the front of the store. "It looks like everything's taken care of." She unlocked the front door to let us out. "Here," she said, handing Carol Ann a sack, "take this warm loaf home with you." She locked the door behind us and waved good-bye.

As we climbed into our car, heady with the aroma of fresh-baked bread, we saw the Fosters' truck pull out of the alley to the side of their shop and head toward the homeless shelter.

"Good people, honest people," I exclaimed. "No wonder Grandpa was willing to convince the bank to lend them the money."

"William," my wife said quietly, "there were only fifty receipts in that envelope."

"Wow, they paid that twenty-five thousand back in just over four years. Their bakery must have been quite successful."

"William, you don't understand. Each of those receipts was for five hundred dollars. The Fosters paid back exactly twenty-five thousand dollars. How do you explain a bank lending that kind of money with no interest?"

Chapter Five

"Do you remember which journal had Malachi's name in it?" I asked my wife once we returned home.

"I'm not sure," she replied. "Let me take a look." She glanced through two or three of the journals before she stopped. "Here," she said, handing the open book to me.

I took the volume from her outstretched hand and spotted Malachi's name halfway down the right-hand page. The entry merely said, "Malachi Foster. Paid in full."

"Not much information," I commented.

"I told you he was a private man," replied my wife.

I picked up the list from beside the telephone and dialed the number following the third name—Portia Adams. The phone rang twice before someone answered it.

"Hello." The voice had a thin, reedy quality.

"Hello. May I speak to Portia Adams?"

"This is she."

I realized that I didn't know whether she was married or not. Was it Miss or Mrs. Adams? "Uh," I said, taking a safe course, "this is William Martin. I believe you worked for my grandfather at the bank."

"That was a long time ago," replied Portia Adams, "a long time ago."

"I . . . we . . . that is, my wife and I are contacting some of his old friends and acquaintances." I paused. "I suppose you heard that he died last summer?"

"Oh, yes," she whispered.

"We're trying to gather some remembrances for my grandmother. I wonder if it would be possible to make an appointment to talk with you for a few minutes?" I waited perhaps ten seconds for a reply. "Ms. Adams?"

"I suppose so," she said quietly. "Although I don't know that I can tell you much about him. It has been a very long time."

"When would it be convenient?" I asked.

"Almost anytime. I don't go out very often." Then, almost as an afterthought, she said, "Could you come to my home? It's a little difficult for me to travel, you know."

"Certainly. Would tomorrow evening about seven o'clock be all right?" I asked.

"That will be fine," she whispered. "Do you know where I live?"

"I have your address."

"Fine," she said with an air of finality. "Good-bye."

"Good-bye."

The air was clear and cold the following night. Christmas lights hung limply across Main Street as we drove toward Portia Adams's home. As we neared the edge of town. I pulled up in front of her house and turned off the car. Strands of twinkling lights decorated the homes on either side of Portia's house, but her home stood starkly undecorated. We walked slowly up the sidewalk to her front porch. A single window to the left of the front door was lighted. The wooden porch creaked beneath my feet as I reached out to press the doorbell. A chime sounded deep within the recesses of the house.

My wife and I stood in the gloom of her porch, watching our breath form clouds in the still winter air. "Maybe we've been stood up," I said after nearly a minute had passed. I reached out to press the doorbell a second time, when the front door opened.

"Are you the Martins?" wheezed Portia Adams from her wheelchair.

"Yes," I replied quickly.

"Well, come in before you freeze to death." She backed her wheelchair away from the door. "If you don't mind, would you push me into the living room?"

Carol Ann and I opened the door wider and entered the foyer. I grasped the handles of the wheelchair and pushed the white-haired, gnarled woman into her living room.

"Sit," she said, waving her hand in the direction of a couch next to the fireplace. The couch, upholstered in a brown velvet, had worn, shiny spots on the arms. A drab afghan had been thrown over the back of it. As we sat down I sank into the cushion until I was nearly sitting on the floor.

A single table lamp lighted the room. The fireplace lay still and cold.

"Thank you for seeing us," began my wife.

"I don't think there's much I can say that will be of interest to you," Portia interjected. "I quit working for your grandfather a long, long time ago. I don't think I've seen him more than a half-dozen times since then." Almost as an afterthought she said, "I'm sorry to hear he died."

"You worked with him at the bank, I understand," said Carol Ann. "He was vice president then, is that right?"

"Oh, no, not at first. He was just a teller. He started just the same as all of us did."

"But you said you worked for him," continued my wife.

"Just for a short time after he became vice president." Her voice trailed off to barely a whisper. "Then I left the bank," she sighed as her head dropped.

"I'd think many people would envy your being able to take an early retirement," said Carol Ann.

Portia Adams's head slowly raised and she stared into my wife's face. "Early retirement? Hardly!"

My wife looked into my face, her forehead wrinkled. I shrugged my shoulders slightly. "That was my under-standing," I interjected. "I always believed you'd retired early."

In the dim light of the table lamp I could see tears forming in Portia's eyes. "That's not quite true," she whispered. A clock somewhere in the house chimed a quarter hour. I sensed that Portia Adams had more to say. My wife cleared her throat and I placed my hand on her arm.

"I was fired." Portia coughed quietly as she reached for a tissue from a box on the lamp table. As her hand moved beneath the beam of the lamp, I could see how terribly knotted and gnarled it was from arthritis. Her voice rose a little in volume. "Fired for doing the same thing every other bank was doing."

"What was that?" I asked, puzzled.

Portia picked at the tissue with her talonlike fingers. "It's so simple today," she began. "Computers do the accounting. In my day we kept a balance sheet for every customer. There was a fairly complicated formula for figuring the check charges each month. It was based on how many checks had been written and how much money was left in the account." She paused and reached for another tissue. "I don't think any of our customers knew the formula we used. We just debited the check charges every month . . . usually three or four dollars."

"You're right," I said, "the computer does make it easier. And they've standardized the charges."

Portia dabbed at her eyes with the tissue. "I just wanted to help the bank make more of a profit. It was so easy."

"What was?" asked my wife.

"I just added a dollar to everyone's check charges. No one ever complained." She lapsed into silence.

"How long did this go on?" I asked.

She stirred in her chair. "Nearly four years," she said at last. Her voice had become husky. "Would you mind getting me a glass of water?" She pointed toward a door that led into a hallway.

"Of course," I said as I tried to rise from the couch. After some difficulty I got to my feet and found my way to the kitchen. I returned a few moments later and handed Portia a glass.

"Thank you," she said, taking the glass from me. She sipped slowly from it and then placed it on the lamp table. "We weren't a very big bank in those days. Not quite three thousand customers. I used to know every one of them by name."

"And where did the money go?" I asked.

"Into the bank's general fund." Her eyes glistened as she looked into mine. "You mustn't think I was doing it for myself. It was for the bank!"

"I understand," my wife said soothingly.

"I can see why no one questioned what you were doing," I said. "And I don't suppose most people realize how much money a dollar per month generates with three thousand accounts."

"I raised over one hundred and ten thousand dollars for the bank during those four years," she said with an element of pride.

"Then what happened?" asked Carol Ann.

Portia's hands pecked at the tissue in her lap. "Then Will Martin became vice president." She paused as if that statement said it all.

"I don't understand," said my wife.

"I had become an account manager. That was a fancy name for a bookkeeper. That's how I was able to manipulate the check charges." She reached for another tissue. "When Will Martin became vice president he started checking the accounts. He was like that, you know, and he found the overcharge." She shifted in her chair. "For three years the auditors hadn't noticed it, but Will Martin did. He found it right off the top."

"And he knew you were responsible?" I asked.

"Not at first. But he started going over all of the accounts and he found out that everyone was charged a dollar too much. He knew I was the only one who figured the charges." She shrugged her shoulders slightly. "So he fired me."

"Just like that?" asked my wife.

"Oh, no," she whispered while she shook her head. "He made it look as if I was leaving for another job. But who retires at thirty years of age?" She twisted her hands around the tissue. "And I knew that everyone in this town knew I'd been fired. I knew that I would never get a job again." She was weeping quietly.

"But why? Why would people think anything of your leaving? People change jobs every day!" exclaimed Carol Ann.

Portia's head hung down, and then in a barely audible voice she said, "Will Martin refunded the money. He sent a letter to every one of our accounts and told them that there had been an accounting error. Everyone in town knew that I'd been in charge of the accounts. Don't you see?"

My wife looked around the living room. Her eyes had grown accustomed to the dimness. There were no pictures of children. "You've never married?"

Portia shook her head. "Will Martin condemned me to prison just as surely as if he'd had me thrown behind bars. I've lived here my whole life." She spread her arms and indicated her home. "My whole life."

I sensed that it was time to leave. I struggled once

again from the couch and extended a hand to my wife. As I pulled her to her feet she said, "You knew every account, didn't you? Every person by name?"

Portia nodded her head. "Every one of them."

"Was there anyone by the name of Lillian who had an account?"

Portia Adams struggled to remember. "Lillian who?"

"I don't know the last name," admitted my wife.

"I'm afraid I can't help you," came the quiet voice. "I'm quite sure that no one named Lillian had an account at the bank."

"Thank you, Miss Adams," I said, extending my hand. She reached up and took it. I felt the knobby fingers within my grasp.

"So much like your grandfather," she said, gazing into my face.

"We'll let ourselves out," said my wife.

Portia Adams looked absentmindedly out the front window as we left her home.

"Still no help with Lillian," said Carol Ann as I let her into the car. "But what a sad old woman."

"Can you find the passage in the journal that led you to her?" I asked. My wife nodded her head.

Shortly after we arrived home, Carol Ann brought me the journal. In my grandfather's careful handwriting I read, "Portia Adams, disappointed."

Chapter Six

I dialed the number my wife had written beside Jorge Castellanas's name. After ten rings I hung up. "No answer?" asked my wife.

I shook my head. "Maybe I ought to try Alicia Cervantes. Her name is next on the list. Oh, I nearly forgot; we don't have a number for her."

"Honey, it's late. Why don't you try again tomorrow?" suggested my wife. "We might not have learned anything about Lillian, but I'm beginning to know your grandfather better."

"So am I," I replied.

We awoke the next morning to a clean, new world. Six inches of snow had fallen during the night. Snowplows had been at work, and the streets were clear. I shoveled the driveway and sidewalk and vowed to buy a snowblower this year.

Half an hour later than usual, I left for my office. As I passed the bank, I noticed that Frank Porter's car was already in its parking place. On a whim I pulled into the parking lot.

I saw him as soon as I entered the bank. "Mr. Porter, might you have a minute for me?" I asked.

Frank Porter had become president of the bank when my grandfather retired. Although Mr. Porter was nearing retirement age himself, my grandfather had handpicked him as his successor. An ample man, he wore a red pin-striped shirt and red tie under his banker-blue three-piece suit. He was completely bald.

He smiled broadly and extended his hand. His hand-shake was firm despite his advanced years. "Certainly, William."

He ushered me into his office and we sat opposite each other at his desk. After a moment or two of small talk, I said, "Mr. Porter, you were here at the bank most of the time my grandfather was here, weren't you?"

"Actually I started working here just before your grandfather was named vice president. Caused quite a shock, you know, because he was so young. But it turned out to be the best decision they could have made." He beamed at me.

I cleared my throat nervously. "Do you remember Portia Adams, by chance?"

Frank Porter tented his fingers together and looked at the wall above my head. "Portia Adams. Portia Adams," he mused. "Oh, yes," he said suddenly. "She was the woman who retired so young. I always envied her."

"Retired? Do you know what happened to her?"

He shook his head. "Nope. She left and, I suppose, moved to Tahiti or somewhere to live on her retirement money."

"She was really given early retirement?"

He nodded his head. "Here, let me call it up on the computer. Although I'm not sure that she's still alive." He turned and pecked away at the keyboard. The screen turned blue and then was flooded with white numbers. "Well, what do you know. She's still alive and she still lives here in town. It looks like we deposit her retirement in her account every month."

"I don't suppose it's very much," I suggested. "I mean, she didn't work for the bank very many years."

Frank Porter pursed his lips. "Pretty substantial, actually. It looks like your grandfather built in a cost-of-living increase that automatically kicks in at the first of the year. I'd say she's able to live pretty comfortably. Especially for someone her age."

"Thanks," I said.

"No problem. Anything else I can do for you?"

I shook my head and rose to my feet. "Well, maybe one other thing. About twenty-two or -three years ago I think the bank loaned some money to a man named Malachi Foster. I wonder if you'd still have the records on that loan."

"Probably not in the computer," said Frank Porter, "but if it's important I can have someone pull it up from the microfilm."

"Would that be a big problem?" I asked.

"Not really. Let me see if I can break someone loose to do it today."

"I don't want to create any problem for you, especially with the Christmas rush."

"No problem," said Frank. "What is it specifically you want to know?"

"The terms of the loan. The interest rate he paid."

"That's easy. If you know the kind of loan, I could check to see what interest rate the bank was charging. All that information's in the computer. We have mortgages that go back that far, you see."

"It was a mortgage, as a matter of fact."

Frank Porter's fingers clicked away at the keys. "Hmmm. Well, Mr. Foster has an account with the bank. I can't reveal the amount, you understand, but I don't see any history of a mortgage loan." He turned in his chair. "If it's paid off, it probably isn't in the computer. Let me do a search today."

"Thanks," I replied.

"I'll give you a call when I know something."

I wished him a merry Christmas and continued the drive to my office. A couple of hours later my wife called on the phone. "Any luck with Jorge?" she asked.

"I haven't had time to call him," I admitted. "I'll try him right now." I hung up the phone, fished the phone number from my shirt pocket, and dialed the number.

"Good morning, J and C Produce," a woman's voice said almost immediately.

"May I speak to Jorge Castellanas?" I asked.

"May I tell him who is calling?"

"William Martin."

"Just one moment, please." I heard a click, and then the sounds of Christmas music filled my ears. *I'm dreaming of a white Christmas* . . . Bing Crosby had nearly finished the song, when a voice interrupted him.

"Hello, this is Jorge. May I help you?"

"Mr. Castellanas, this is William Martin. I believe you

knew my grandfather, Will Martin." I continued the explanation I had concocted about gathering information for my grandmother.

"Yes, I knew him. He was a good man. I am so sorry to hear that he passed away this last summer. But I knew so little about him. I am not certain I can help you very much."

"Perhaps we could meet for a few minutes. I'm sure it wouldn't take long," I ventured.

"Of course. Could I interest you in lunch?"

I glanced at my day planner. "Lunch would be fine," I replied.

"If you don't mind coming to our warehouse, I could have something brought in. We're quite busy at this season of the year, as you might imagine."

"Sounds good to me. What time would you like me there?" I glanced at my watch; it was eleven thirty.

"How soon can you get away?" he asked.

"Right now, if it's convenient," I replied.

"Fine. I'll see you in a few minutes. Good-bye."

I opened the phone book and looked up the address of J and C Produce. It was located on the edge of town next to the railroad tracks. "I'm going to lunch," I told my secretary. "I'll be back in a couple of hours."

The clouds had disappeared and the fresh snow sparkled in the sunlight. The first street I drove down ended at a chain-link enclosure. After only one more miscue I arrived at J and C Produce. The building occupied most of a city block. Four railroad cars were parked on the track next to the west side of the building. I was amazed I hadn't paid attention to it before.

I entered the lobby at the southeast corner of the building, where a small bird of a woman sat behind a desk typing on a keyboard. Her black hair was streaked with gray, and a pair of half-moon glasses perched on her thin, pointed nose. She turned in her chair and looked over the tops of the glasses at me as I entered. Her bright red lips formed a thin line. "Yes?"

I handed her my card. "William Martin to see Mr. Castellanas."

She took my card between her finger and thumb and inspected it, then pushed down a button beside her telephone. "Jorge, your lunch appointment's here," she said in a melodious voice. Without another word she turned back to her keyboard.

I inspected the office while I waited. A clock was mounted on the wall near the door and periodically emitted a whir and a click. Next to it was a calendar from Union Pacific Railroad showing a train traveling through snow-covered fields. Above the receptionist's desk was a reproduction of an oil painting showing a number of workers in a field. I tried to remember who had painted it . . . Van Gogh stuck in my mind.

Suddenly the door next to the desk flew open and a huge bear of a man entered the room. "Mr. Martin, I am Jorge," he greeted me. He was clothed in denim pants and a red flannel shirt covered with a rubber apron. "Come, come with me. Lunch will be here soon." He winked at the receptionist, who seemed not to notice, although I saw a flicker of a smile on her lips.

I followed him through the doorway into the warehouse of J and C Produce. Nearly fifty men and women were unloading the railroad freight cars from open bays on the west side of the building. The aroma of mingled fruit filled the air. "You have quite an operation here," I said as I hurried to keep up with my host.

"Normally we have the fruit unloaded before sunup," he replied, "but at this season we get slowed up a bit trying to get all the orders filled." We walked the length of the building before we entered his office. The only furniture in it was a small desk with two chairs and a green couch upholstered in Naugahyde. There was a split in one arm of the couch, and white, matted stuffing showed. "Not very fancy," he apologized with a grin. He pulled a chair up to the desk. "Please, have a seat. As I said, lunch will be here soon."

I sat down and Jorge Castellanas dropped his bulk into the chair behind the desk. He ran his hands through his shaggy black hair and locked his fingers behind his neck. "Now, how can I help you?" He put his feet up on his desk.

"I'm just trying to gather some information about my grandfather for my grandmother. Your name appeared in one of his journals and I'm just really grasping at straws, I guess."

"Must be an old journal. I haven't had anything to do with your grandfather in about twenty-five years. I knew about him, of course. Big banker, insurance man, you know, but I haven't had any reason to see him since he helped my family get the water for our vineyard.".

My forehead wrinkled. "I guess I don't know anything about that," I confessed.

"Get your feet off the desk!" commanded the

receptionist. She entered the little room with two white paper bags in her hands. Jorge complied with a sheepish grin.

She left the bags on the desk and retreated toward the door. "Thanks, sweet thing," he said. "William, you've met my wife, haven't you?" I nodded as the door shut behind her. "Ham or turkey?" he asked, indicating the bags.

"Uh, turkey, if you don't mind." I opened the proffered paper bag and found a sandwich made of thick slabs of turkey on sourdough bread.

"Dig in and I'll tell you about how your grandpappy helped my family." He pulled out his ham sandwich and wrenched off a mouthful with his gleaming white teeth.

"About twenty-five years ago my family had an orchard and a vineyard out in the foothills to the west of town. We grew our own apricots, peaches, plums, and cherries in the orchard and had a couple hundred grapevines. Next to our forty acres the Julianos owned about two hundred acres of cheatgrass and scrub that they'd never done anything with. Well, Old Man Juliano died and his two boys didn't want the land. I think they wanted the money, really. Anyway, my family made an offer to buy their spread. There was only one problem. They didn't have any water rights for the land. And we didn't have enough shares to water any more than our forty acres." He took another huge bite of sandwich and chewed thoughtfully for a minute.

"My father, God rest his soul, was still alive, and he made an application with the Lambert Hollow Water District to see if we could buy some more water shares. They turned him down flat. I'm not here to say they were prejudiced or anything, but Papa spoke with quite an accent and . . . well, you know how some people are. Anyway, Papa sent me to see your grandpappy. He was a trustee on the water board, or something like that. Papa trusted him completely. So I went to see him and I asked for his help. He listened to my story and then went with me to look at the land."

He took a deep drink from the bottle of grape juice that had been delivered with the sandwich. "He walked up to the top of the rise and ran his fingers through the dirt. 'Ought to be productive, if you can get water,' he said. Well, we didn't hear anything from him for about two weeks. I'd about given up hope of getting the land, and then your grandpappy showed up at our house. He and Papa talked for a while and then they invited me into the room. 'Will says they not gonna give us no water,' my Papa said, 'but they gonna let us drill a well, if we think it's worth it.'"

I swallowed my piece of turkey sandwich. "So, did you dig the well?"

"My family was divided. Papa wanted to buy the land and dig the well. I wasn't quite so sure. It costs a lot to dig a well, and if we didn't find water, we'd have spent a lot of money and had two hundred useless acres of land. It was a big risk. We argued about it for several days; then the pressure really got turned up. The Juliano boys got another offer for the land. They gave us three days to decide." He paused and took another bite of his sandwich.

"And?"

He swallowed and took another swig of grape juice.

"Papa sent me to see your grandpappy again. 'Go ask Will,' he said, 'and take his advice.' So I went to the bank and asked him. We sat in his office and he put his elbows on his desk and put his hands together like he was praying and leaned his chin on his thumbs. He stared at me for a long time and then he said, 'Do it, Jorge; you'll never be sorry.'"

He finished off the bottle of grape juice. "He was right. We bought the land and drilled the well. By spring we had two hundred more acres of grapevines planted. We hit water less than thirty feet deep, plenty of water to take care of our vineyard."

He wadded up his napkin and dropped it into the paper bag with the empty juice bottle. "I haven't had occasion to see your grandpappy since then."

"Thank you, Jorge," I said. "Thanks for the information about my grandfather, and thanks for lunch. That was a great sandwich."

"How did you like the grape juice?" He flashed a gleaming smile.

"Wonderful. Where did you get it?" I looked at the label: "Juliano's Sparkling Grape Juice."

"We bottle it ourselves. We used the Juliano label to honor the family from whom we bought the land. Of course, now we own quite a bit more land." He shrugged his shoulders. "I guess we have quite a bit to thank Will Martin for, after all."

He opened the door and we started back across the warehouse. The freight cars had been unloaded and pallets of fruit were stacked neatly.

"I have one more question, if you don't mind," I said.

"Shoot."

"Among the people I'm trying to locate is a woman named Lillian. Does that strike a chord with you?"

Jorge rubbed his chin. "I don't believe I know anyone named Lillian. Do you know her last name?"

"No," I said, "just Lillian."

"Sorry," he said, shaking his head. He opened the door to the small reception room. His wife sat at her keyboard. "Thanks for lunch, angel baby," he said.

Chapter Seven

The clouds had gathered again as I drove back to work. My secretary handed me several phone messages when I returned to the agency. The third one was from Frank Porter at the bank. I dialed the number. "First National. How may I direct your call?"

"This is William Martin returning a call to Mr. Porter," I replied.

"One moment please." *Angels we have heard on high, sweetly singing o'er the plains.*

"William, thanks for calling back so quickly. I just wanted you to know I had Mary search the microfilm record for Malachi Foster. Can't find anywhere that he ever had a loan from the bank. Sorry I can't be of more help."

"I appreciate your time, Mr. Porter. Have a merry Christmas."

"You too, my boy. It was no trouble at all."

The rest of my afternoon was taken up with meetings. As I was getting ready to leave for the day, the phone rang. "Good afternoon, William Martin."

"Sweetheart, did you have any success getting hold of Jorge Castellanas?" asked my wife.

"I did. I'll tell you about it when I get home. But no help with Lillian."

"How long are you going to be?"

"I was just leaving when you called. I'll be right home."

"See you soon. Oh, I found a phone number for Alicia Cervantes."

Huge snowflakes were falling as I started the car and drove toward home. The Christmas lights twinkled brightly along Main Street. I realized that Christmas was just three weeks away and I hadn't finished shopping for my wife, nor had I gotten my grandmother her present.

By the time I pulled into our driveway it was clear that we were in for a major storm. I hurried into the warmth of our kitchen. Carol Ann greeted me at the door as she had every day of our three-year marriage. "Dinner's ready. Let's sit down and then you can tell me about your day."

Over dinner I told her about my lunchtime experience with Jorge Castellanas and what I'd learned about Portia Adams and Malachi Foster.

"But still no Lillian," said my wife. "Well, at least I've located Alicia Cervantes, only it's Blackburn now."

"Blackburn? Did she marry Rudy Blackburn?" I wondered out loud.

"Could be. You told me that they used to live next door. I went over and talked to Mrs. Colburn and she told me that the Cervantes had moved over to Mount Fillmore. I called information and found there were only two Cervantes families in the community. I got lucky. The first phone call was Alicia's mother. She told me that Alicia lives in Copper City and that her name is Blackburn. She gave me her address and phone number."

"You're quite the detective," I said, smiling. "Copper City is only an hour's drive away. Let's see if we can set up an appointment with Alicia Blackburn."

A gust of wind drove the snow against the kitchen window. "Don't make it for tonight," warned my wife.

I placed the phone call and waited while it rang several times. I was just about to hang up when someone picked up the phone. "Hello," said the tired voice.

"Could I speak to Alicia Blackburn?" I asked.

"This is she."

"Alicia, this is William Martin, your old next-door neighbor. Do you remember me?"

"Of course I remember you." There was wariness in her voice. "What do you want?"

"I'm trying to gather some information about my grandfather. My wife and I wonder if we could set up an appointment to visit you for a few minutes and collect your remembrances of him."

"You haven't moved, have you? We live in Copper City, you know."

"No, we haven't moved, but we're willing to drive down to your place if you can give us a few minutes of your time."

"That's a long way to come. I don't know that I can help you much. Your grandfather was just a next-door neighbor. I didn't have much to do with him, except . . ." I could hear the reluctance in her voice. "I guess it would be all right. When do you want to come?"

"We've got a pretty good snowstorm settling in on us.

What if we came Sunday afternoon, after church. Would that be all right? Say three o'clock."

"Sure, that's fine. It's good to hear from you, William. See you Sunday."

The snow swirled around the house as I hung up the phone. "I don't think she's really excited to see us," I said to my wife. "I wonder why?"

She shrugged her shoulders. "Start a fire in the fireplace, will you? I have a feeling we're going to want to stay inside tonight."

By morning a foot of fresh snow covered the driveway. It took nearly an hour to dig my way out. A snowblower moved from my list of wants to my list of needs. That afternoon we had a few more snow flurries but by Sunday the roads were clear. Carol Ann and I climbed into our car and headed for Copper City. She slipped a tape into the cassette player and we listened to Christmas carols as we made our way down the highway. Copper City was still rural enough that no freeway served the town.

"Tell me what you know about Alicia," said my wife.

"She's two years younger than I," I began. "Pretty as a picture and smart as a whip, as her dad used to say. I think she was the prom queen the year after I graduated from high school." I struggled to remember much about her. "I think every boy in school had a crush on her, and I suspect she left a trail of broken hearts behind. She was really smart. I think she took a couple of advanced placement classes as a sophomore. She always talked about being a doctor, but to be honest, I haven't kept track of her since I graduated and her family moved."

We drove on through whipped-cream-covered pines and aspens until we reached our destination. Copper City was built for one purpose—to service a copper smelter that provided its major employment. The snow was covered with a gray dusting from the huge smokestacks that rose high above the hip of the hill west of town. My wife looked again at the address: 116 Virginia Street. We drove slowly down the main street of town.

"Virginia must run parallel to Main Street," said my wife.

We had reached the south end of town. We turned east a block and retraced our route to the north. When we reached Center Street we turned east again and drove until we ran out of streets. We had not found Virginia Street. "It's almost three o'clock. Maybe we'd better find someone and ask," said Carol Ann.

I made a U-turn and drove west. When we reached Main Street, two young men were leaning against a pickup truck parked near the intersection. I rolled down my window. "Excuse me, could you tell me where Virginia Street is?"

"Just keep going," said one of the boys. He removed his cowboy hat and pointed down the road with it. "It's about four or five more blocks."

I thanked him and we drove across Main Street until we found Virginia Street. At last we spotted the house: it was perhaps seventy-five years old, with a badly sagging front porch running the full width of it. The house was greatly in need of a coat of paint. The shingles on the roof showed multi-colored patches.

I helped my wife from the car and we started toward the front door. The wooden steps had broken boards, and I jumped up on the porch and helped my wife. The floor creaked ominously beneath our weight. I raised my hand to knock on the door, when a voice called from the side of the house.

"William, around here. We live in the basement apartment."

Chapter Eight

I helped my wife down from the porch and we made our way through the gray-crusted snow to a pathway that had been tramped down by the side of the house. Alicia Cervantes Blackburn stood shivering in the cold. She had a faded green bathrobe pulled around her thin frame. She clutched it closed with one hand while she beckoned with the other. "This way. I've been watching for you. It's good to see you again, William."

"Carol Ann, this is Alicia, my old next-door neighbor," I said as we carefully descended the ice-covered steps.

"Pleased to meet you," said Alicia. "Have a seat." She indicated a threadbare couch. I moved a stack of clothing to one end of the couch and we sat down.

Alicia perched on a chair across the room. I could hear a child whimpering softly in another room. It was hard to believe that I was looking at the same girl who had won the hearts of the entire school. Her skin was sallow and her cheeks were sunken. Her eyes stared out of dark caverns. Her hair hung limply to her shoulders. "So," she said, "how long have the two of you been married?"

"Almost three years," I replied.

"Any children?"

"Not yet," said Carol Ann. "We keep hoping."

"I've got three," said Alicia, jerking her head toward the sound we could hear. "Ruth, Randy, and Little Rudy." She pulled the bathrobe tighter against her thin frame. It was cold in the room.

"How old are they?" asked my wife.

"Ruth's six, Randy's three, and the baby's six months."

I wondered why we didn't get to meet them. "So you married Rudy Blackburn," I said.

Alicia nodded her head. "Yup. He's at work over at the smelter. He gets off at six."

"Does he like it?" asked Carol Ann.

"Hates it," said Alicia, "but at least it's a job."

It was getting harder for me to remember what Alicia had looked like in high school. I realized she was only twenty-six years of age, but my eyes told me she was an old woman.

"You wanted to talk about your grandpa, is that right?" she said.

We nodded our heads in unison. "He died last summer, and we're gathering some memories of him for my grandmother," I began. "Your name appeared in his journal, and that led us here."

"I'm amazed you could find me," she said, shaking her head.

"My wife found you," I replied.

"Like I told you on the phone, your grandfather was just our next-door neighbor. I mean, he was a really nice old man, but I didn't have much to do with him. I'm sorry

55

you had to drive all this way just for that, but I don't know what else I can say."

"You don't remember anything special about him?" asked Carol Ann.

Alicia gazed out the window above our heads. "He tried to help me get a scholarship, but he failed."

"Why don't you tell us about it," said my wife.

There was a long pause. In the silence we could hear the quiet cry of the baby. "It was my senior year," she began, "and I had plans to go to college and become a doctor. I knew my family couldn't afford to help me with tuition, but I had taken six advanced placement courses and figured that would help me. One Tuesday morning my counselor called me into his office—you remember Mr. Barton, don't you?" I nodded my head. "He said I was eligible to compete for one of five scholarships that paid full tuition, books, and living expenses for four years. And if I kept my grades up, it would help me through medical school. The scholarship was sponsored by Phillips Petroleum, and since Dad worked there, I was eligible. The application was about twenty pages long. I asked Mr. Barton how many people were competing and he told me I was one of ten." Her dull eyes had taken on a shine as she remembered the experience.

"Sounds like quite a scholarship," I said.

She nodded her head. "I went home and told my mom and dad about it. I was certain that I'd be one of the five. After all, I had a 4.0 grade point average and six AP classes. I put the application on top of the television set where I'd be sure to see it." Her eyes began to mist.

"What happened?" asked Carol Ann.

"Well, the next day my mom tried to get me to fill out the application. It was so long and it asked for so many little written responses that I told her I didn't know how to fill it out. She called your grandfather and asked if he'd have time to help me. He came over that Wednesday afternoon and sat down with me. He tried to explain what I needed to write, but it was late and I was going out on a date, so I didn't pay as much attention as I should have. Finally he said, 'If you just do what I've told you, you'll be a shoe-in.'"

"Then what happened?" I asked.

"I was so excited that I forgot to look at the date the application was due. You see, Mr. Barton had waited till the last minute to get the application to me. How was I to know that I needed to fill it out and mail it in by Thursday?" She clutched the bathrobe tightly and gazed out the narrow window.

"Monday morning Mr. Barton asked me if I'd gotten the application filled out, and I told him I'd get it done that afternoon. That's when I learned it might be too late." Alicia gave an involuntary shudder.

"I went home and told Mom and Dad. They called your grandfather to see what he could do to help. He was the superintendent or something."

"A member of the school board," I replied.

"Whatever. Anyway, he told me to hurry and get the application in. I filled it out. It took nearly three hours. Then Rudy drove me down to Phillips to turn it in. They told me it was due the Friday before. So I went home and told my dad. He went over and got your grandfather to see if he could do anything more."

"And you say he failed?" Carol Ann asked.

Alicia nodded her head. "He took it the next day to the refinery and tried to plead my case. I guess they wouldn't listen to him. They just said they had a rule they had to stick by. The only consolation was that four other girls didn't get theirs turned in either."

"Didn't you apply for any other scholarships?" I asked.

She shook her head. "Nope. Besides, Rudy was pressuring me to marry him as soon as I graduated, and he didn't want me going off to college. It's probably better this way." She gave a resigned sigh.

"When did you get married?" asked Carol Ann.

Alicia looked down at the threadbare carpet. "My folks didn't want us to get married. That's why they sold the house and moved to Mount Fillmore. But that didn't stop Rudy and me. We got married that summer, just before I turned nineteen."

The baby in the other room began to cry more loudly. "I've got to feed the baby," she said. "It was good to see you again."

I helped my wife up from the couch. A little girl peered around a doorway in the direction from which the crying had come. "Mom, Rudy needs to be fed," she whispered quietly. The little girl had her mother's dark hair and the same sunken eyes. Suddenly a little boy's head poked around his sister's arm.

"These must be your children," exclaimed Carol Ann. "They're precious."

Alicia smiled wanly. The two children moved into the

front room. Both were wearing only underwear. Dark bruises were visible on their arms.

"Are they all right?" my wife asked Alicia with concern.

"They're fine," said Alicia. "Sometimes they get out of hand and Rudy has to discipline them. That's all." She pushed the two children back into the kitchen. "I've got to feed the baby," she said flatly. I could see the tears coursing down her cheeks.

We drove home through the snow-covered hills in silence. From the tape player came the subdued strains of *Peace on earth, good will to men.*

The Christmas lights twinkled brightly overhead as we made our way down Main Street and to our house. "William, we forgot to ask her about Lillian."

I nodded my head. "I know, I know."

Chapter Nine

"What are we going to do?" asked my wife. "We can't just ignore that family. Those children are being abused. And I suspect Alicia is too."

I nodded my head. "I know." I picked up the phone and dialed information. "I need the number for the family service center in Copper City," I said when the operator answered. "I see. Thank you. Could you give me that number?" I wrote it down and hung up the phone. "Apparently they're served by a county agency in Brewerton. I'll try their number."

I dialed the number I'd been given. There was no answer. "I'll have to try them tomorrow." I hung up the phone and then dialed my grandmother's number.

"Hello, Martin's residence."

"Hi, Grandmother. I just thought we ought to check up on you."

"Thank you, dear. I'm just fine." After a brief pause she said, "I tried calling earlier. I guess you were out."

"Carol Ann and I drove over to Copper City after dinner."

"Copper City?"

"Still trying to get your Christmas present, Grandma," I said.

"And still no luck?" she asked.

"Now, you know better than to ask about a Christmas gift, don't you?" I tried to keep a lightness in my voice that I did not feel.

"Well, give my love to Carol Ann." She hung up. I walked to the window and looked out on the crystal clear winter night.

"Who's next on the list?" asked my wife.

I went to the desk and pulled the folded page from behind the telephone. "Wendel Walker."

I started a fire in the fireplace to take the chill from the room. The flames flickered brightly.

"Tell me what you know about him, sweetheart."

I scratched my head. "He worked for Grandpa at the insurance agency. I thought he was an old man when I first met him, and that's been at least twenty years ago. He was always such a friendly man. One thing I remember is that he used to have a bowl of mints on his desk, and when I'd go into his office he'd let me take one of them."

"What's happened to him?"

I shrugged my shoulders. "I really don't know. I can't remember when he retired or left the agency. It was growing quite fast and quite a number of new agents were coming on board. I'm really surprised he's still alive. He must be close to ninety years of age."

"Well," said my wife, "let's hope he can lead us to Lillian."

I nodded my head and gazed into the fire. My wife

curled up in front of the fireplace with a book in her lap. I rested my hand on her shoulder and thought how I blessed I was to have such a good woman to share my life. The memory of Alicia Blackburn kept flashing into my mind's eye. I shook my head.

Monday dawned gray and overcast. The predictions of another storm seemed accurate. I donned an overcoat, kissed my wife good-bye, and started for the agency. Before I had driven a block, a light snow began to fall, and an hour later the snowplows were clearing the roads.

When I reached my office, I dialed the Brewerton phone number. "Williams County Social Services, how may I help you?" The voice was cheery and bright.

I was a little unsure how to begin. "Uh, yesterday my wife and I were visiting a friend—well, an acquaintance—in Copper City, and we think that maybe there's a possibility that the children are being abused." I drew in a breath.

"Could I have your name, sir? It will be kept strictly confidential."

Do I really want to get involved? I thought. *How do I explain why we were there? Maybe I ought to just hang up.*

"Sir?" the voice questioned.

I realized I had been holding my breath. I let it out slowly. "William Martin," I replied.

"I realize this may be difficult, Mr. Martin," soothed the voice. "I also need your phone number."

"My home phone is 555-4385," I replied. "Usually my wife is there, if I'm not."

"I understand, Mr. Martin. Now, what is the name of the family you're concerned about?"

I told the faceless voice what Carol Ann and I had observed the previous day.

"Thank you, Mr. Martin, but I need to know the name of the family involved."

"Blackburn. Alicia Blackburn and her children. Her husband's name is . . ."

"Rudy," said the voice somewhat more quietly. "We're well aware of the family, Mr. Martin. I'll put this information in their file and we'll make another contact."

"Is there anything else that can be done?"

"We're trying to get Mr. and Mrs. Blackburn into some counseling," answered the voice, "but they seem quite reluctant."

"I'm really concerned about them."

The voice softened. "We're all concerned, Mr. Martin. We'll see what we can do. Thank you for your call."

"You're welcome." I hung up the phone as a vision of Alicia Blackburn swam before my eyes. I shook my head and pulled the folded list of names from my pocket. I dialed the number following Wendel Walker's name.

"Hello." The faint voice sounded frail and feminine.

"Hello, is Wendel Walker there by chance?"

"Mentally he's here on occasion," she chuckled sadly and softly.

"Is he there now? This is William Martin at the insurance agency where he used to work."

"William Martin? Oh, Will's grandson, aren't you?"

"That's right. I'd just like to visit with Wendel for a

few minutes if I can arrange an appointment. To whom am I speaking?"

"This is his daughter, Annie. Well, he's home most all the time. At his age you don't go out a whole lot, but most of the time his mind isn't too sharp. You know what I mean?"

"Is there a time when I could drop by and talk to him? Sometime that would be better than another?"

Annie thought for a moment. "Well, he's usually more alert in the morning. Any chance you could come by before noon?"

I looked at my appointment calendar. Monday and Tuesday mornings were filled. "How about Wednesday, about ten o'clock? Would that be a possibility?"

"As good a day as any," chuckled Annie. She gave me their address.

"Thank you. I'll see you Wednesday."

As I hung up the phone, my secretary buzzed me. My first appointment of the day was waiting.

Chapter Ten

Wednesday morning showed definite improvement over the past two days. The snow had stopped falling, and only high, thin clouds masked the sun. At fifteen minutes before ten I left the agency and started toward the address I'd been given for Wendel Walker.

The home was in an older section of town, but the houses lining the street were well maintained. The front porch of the Walker home was supported by white columns that were wrapped with Christmas lights. The walk had been shoveled clear of snow. As I walked toward the house, my breath hung in the air. "Apartment for Rent," proclaimed a neatly lettered sign in the front window.

The doorbell responded with the sound of Westminster chimes from deep within the house. I could hear approaching footsteps, and the door opened to reveal a bright-eyed, white-haired woman of about seventy years. "Mr. Martin, I presume," she said, pushing the storm door open with one hand and extending the other toward me.

"Yes," I replied, taking her hand. "And you must be"—it didn't seem right for me to call her by her first name—"Wendel Walker's daughter."

Her eyes fairly danced as she looked at me. "Yes, his oldest daughter, but please call me Annie." She smiled a bright smile and pulled me into the house. "You must be half frozen," she said as she shut the door behind us.

"It is a bit cold," I admitted.

"Just put your coat over that chair," she said, pointing into the dining room on the right side of the entry. "Daddy's in here." She led me into the living room on the left. "He's in fairly good shape this morning." She gave a low, melodious chuckle.

Wendel Walker sat in a rocking chair in the living room with a checkered quilt gathered across his lap. He had lost so much weight that he looked almost skeletal. Sparse strands of white hair stuck up wildly on his head. As I approached him he attempted to rise from the chair.

"Don't get up for me, Mr. Walker," I said, extending my hand.

"Couldn't if he wanted to," chuckled his daughter.

Wendel Walker held out his hand, and I took it gently in mine. His skin was almost translucent, and his hand was cold to the touch. He looked at me with cloudy blue eyes rimmed in red. "Do I know you?" he wheezed softly.

Before I could answer, his daughter said quite loudly, "This is Will Martin's grandson, Daddy."

"Who?" he said as he turned toward his daughter's voice.

"Will Martin's grandson," her voice boomed out. "You remember Will from your office."

"Will Martin." He seemed to be searching for the name in the recesses of his memory. Suddenly his face lit up. "Will Martin. Will from the agency." He pulled my face closer to his. "You're not Will Martin. You're too young."

Annie leaned close to her father's ear. "This is Will's grandson, Daddy. But his name's Will too."

He wrinkled his forehead. "He's too young to be Will." He let go of my hand and shrank back against his rocking chair. "Too young." He closed his eyes.

"I'm sorry," said his daughter. "Daddy's getting quite forgetful. He's nearly ninety-five, you know."

"It's good of you to take care of him," I said.

She smiled. "Well, he took good care of all of us for a lot of years."

"How many children did he have?"

"Eight. I'm the oldest, and my youngest brother would have been sixty next February." She glanced at her father, walked over to his side, and arranged the blanket. Wendel was now snoring softly. "I'm afraid Daddy's not going to be much help, William. Is there anything I can do for you?"

"Well, maybe. You probably know that my grandfather passed away rather suddenly last summer." She nodded and motioned me toward a couch. I sat down on one end and she seated herself on the other.

"I'm trying to gather some information about him for my grandmother," I told her.

Annie smiled a thin little smile. "I've often wished we'd done that for Daddy. Mom died nearly twenty years ago and we talked about putting something together, but just never got around to it. After Roy died—he was my youngest brother—we just sort of put other things first."

"I'm sorry," I said.

Annie looked over at her sleeping father. "I'm the only one left. Daddy outlived all the others." She paused a moment. "Funny, isn't it—the oldest child outliving all her brothers and sisters. But then, somebody had to take care of him."

"I don't imagine it's easy," I replied.

"Oh, most days it isn't too bad. And after he goes, I'll be all alone." Her voice had grown soft and wistful. "There's even an apartment downstairs, but it's been vacant for a while. I'll be alone again, just like when my Joseph died." She smoothed her skirt with both hands.

"I'm sorry," I said again.

Annie looked at me and sighed. "Well, nothing can be done about it now." Wendel snored softly from his rocking chair. She looked in his direction again. "Of course, your grandfather's to blame," she said, smiling. "Daddy wouldn't be here if it weren't for him."

"I don't understand," I blurted.

"You don't know what your grandfather did for Daddy?"

I shook my head. "Please, tell me."

"It was, let's see"—she started counting on her fingers—"twenty-five years ago last month. Daddy was working late one night at the agency with your grandfather, and he had a pain in his shoulder and chest. He thought it was just heartburn, but your grandfather insisted on taking him to the hospital. Daddy was having a heart attack, and they said that had he gone much longer . . . well, we could have lost him." She gazed fondly at the old man in the rocking chair.

I started to speak, but she held up her hand. "That's not all. They were doing a new technique with bypass surgery and they wanted to do it with Daddy, but because it was so experimental it wasn't covered by insurance. The doctors were sure that it would let Daddy live a normal life, but the cost was astronomical. Without it, they gave him a year or two to live. We just gave up hope as a family. There was no way we could afford the surgery. Then your grandfather went to the home office. I don't know how he did it, but he persuaded them to cover Daddy's surgery."

Wendel's eyes opened slowly and he blinked a few times.

"Do you need something, Daddy?" Annie yelled at him.

He smiled wanly and slowly shook his head. His eyes closed again.

"After Daddy recovered he went back to work for your grandfather for a few more years until he retired. And as you can see, he's still with us." She smiled. "At least his heart's going strong, even if his mind isn't. So, as I said, your grandfather's to blame."

"Thank you for sharing that with me. I had no idea."

"We were so sorry to hear about your grandfather passing away," said Annie. "He was such a good man. I can't believe he ever had an enemy in the world." She stood up. "Is there anything else?" The interview was clearly over.

"Just one thing, if I might ask. Do you know of anyone named Lillian who was connected with the agency in any way?"

"Lillian?" She screwed up her face in thought. "I can't remember Daddy ever mentioning anyone by that name. I'm sorry, is it important?"

"Just a thought," I answered. "Please say good-bye to your father for me."

His head had slumped to one side and he was snoring more loudly.

Annie led me to the front door. "Please don't be afraid to come again," she said. "We don't have many visitors anymore."

"Thank you. And merry Christmas."

The door shut behind me and I felt the cold air slap my face as I hurried to the car.

Chapter Eleven

"One week until Christmas, and still no Lillian," I said to my wife as we ate dinner.

"Well, don't give up hope. We still have four names to go. Do you want me to see if Amanda Grossbeck is home?"

"That's the next name, isn't it? Our old neighbor from across the street. Sure, we might as well strike out twice in one day."

"Don't sound so discouraged, William. I'm just certain we're going to be able to give your grandmother her Christmas gift."

My wife consulted the list of names and dialed the phone. "Mrs. Grossbeck? This is Carol Ann Martin. You don't know me, but I married William Martin, Will Martin's grandson." She paused. "Yes, that's right, from across the street. Yes. Mrs. Grossbeck, is there any time that William and I could visit with you? He's trying to put some remembrances of his grandfather together for his grandmother for Christmas."

My wife smiled at me across the kitchen; then a frown crossed her face. "I see, when are you leaving? In the morning? I suppose it would be out of the question to suggest we visit you briefly tonight?" Another pause. "Oh, no more than ten minutes. We'll be right over. Thank you."

Carol Ann hung up the phone. "Get your coat, sweetheart; we need to go right now. She's leaving town in the morning. It's lucky we called her tonight."

Ten minutes later we were standing in front of Amanda Grossbeck's home. Every tree in the yard was covered with twinkling lights. A huge wreath of fragrant pine boughs hung on the door. I rang the doorbell. We heard footsteps approaching and the door was flung open by a smiling elf of a woman dressed all in red, with a white neckerchief around her throat that was held in place with a gold pin shaped like Santa Claus.

"You must be the Martins. Come in, come in." We entered a room filled with Christmas decorations. A snow-white tree stood in one corner of the living room, covered with tiny gold trumpets, harps, and violins. The mantel was draped in pine boughs, and two dozen differently shaped candles were arranged between the boughs and the mirror that hung above the fireplace. A pile of brightly wrapped packages was on a low table to one side of the Christmas tree. The room was filled with the delicious odor of pine and cinnamon.

"Please, please be seated," she said. "Let me take your coats. Oh, but it's a cold night out there." We sat down on an elegant love seat. Amanda Grossbeck scurried through a doorway with our coats and returned quickly. "Would you like some hot cider? It's an old family recipe." Without waiting for an answer, she disappeared through another door and returned shortly with three steaming cups of cider on a cut-glass tray. The cider smelled wonderful.

"Now, what can I do for you? I'm sorry I'm in such a hurry, but I've got to get packed. I leave just before nine o'clock in the morning." She inhaled the aroma of the cider and then took a sip.

"Well," said Carol Ann, "as I mentioned on the phone, William's trying to gather some information about his grandfather to give to his grandmother for Christmas."

Amanda nodded her head. "He was a good man, Will was, a good man."

I could tell my wife was having as much trouble as I had had in figuring out how to ask about Lillian.

"How long did you live across the street, Mrs. Grossbeck?"

"Oh, call me Amanda, dear. We lived there, oh, let's see, from the time we got married until 1975. That's nearly twenty years, I guess."

"And then you moved here? Is that right?"

"Yes, dear, I moved here, and Victoria—that's my sister—she moved to Fargo."

"I understand you and your sister—"

"Victoria," interrupted Amanda.

"Yes, Victoria—you lived next door to each other, is that right?" asked my wife.

"That's right. Straight across the street from your—well, his—grandfather. Well, and then, of course, William came to live with them. You've grown up, William; I didn't recognize you when you came to the door." She smiled in my direction. "Of course, you were a little boy when we moved, so I guess that's understandable."

"Why did you move?" asked my wife.

A cloud crossed Amanda Grossbeck's face. "Because of the fence."

"The fence?" I said.

"The fence," repeated Amanda.

"I don't understand," said my wife.

"The fence that ran between Victoria's house and mine. She wanted to take it down after Robert and Daniel died. And I wanted it left up. I mean, good fences make good neighbors, don't you know."

"Robert was your husband?" asked Carol Ann softly.

"Maybe I should just tell you the whole story. My goodness, we'll have to hurry though; I've got to get packed." She sipped from her cup of cider. "When Victoria and I were growing up, she always liked to boss me around. She's barely a year older than I, but she liked to think she was the boss. Anyway, when we were in high school we started dating these two boys who were the best of friends. Robert Grossbeck and Daniel Middleton were the heartthrobs of Ralph Waldo Emerson High School. Victoria couldn't decide which one she liked better, but she finally settled on Daniel. Of course, that suited me just fine because I thought Robert Grossbeck was the handsomest man on the face of this earth." Her face fairly shone with a beaming smile and twinkling eyes.

"Mother and Father weren't too pleased that we were going steady with these two boys when Victoria was a senior and I was just a junior, but we didn't care. We were in love. Father was especially concerned with Daniel because he wasn't of our faith. I think that just made Victoria more determined to marry him, and she started going to church with him. Besides, we weren't all that reli-gious anyway. I went to church a couple of times a year, and it didn't seem like any big thing to me." She looked at her watch. "Oh, my gracious, I've got to speed this story up.

"Well, to make this long story a little shorter, we had a double wedding two weeks after I graduated from high school. Robert and Daniel had found these two little houses, starter homes they called them, right across the street from your grandfather's house. We moved into them and were just as happy as could be." Her voice was cheerful, as if she were reliving these moments. Suddenly she became somber. "Then the Korean War took Robert and Daniel away from us . . . forever. The letters inform-ing us of their deaths arrived two days apart. I was just trying to help Victoria recover from the shock of Daniel's loss, when my own letter was delivered."

She stopped her narrative and took a deep drink of the fragrant cider. "Suddenly the Church became more important in our lives. We hoped, we struggled for some explanation as to why two strong, handsome young men had to be taken in the prime of their lives. If there was a God, how could he let such a thing happen? At first we sought comfort in each other's misery, but then we began to draw apart. Victoria began to seek comfort in Daniel's church. I turned to my own. We began to argue as to which religion was right. Our arguments went on for years. I came to understand that God hadn't killed Robert and that he gave us the right to live our own lives and either gain the reward or pay the price for our actions. Then Victoria decided she wanted to take down the fence between us. I refused and she became totally unreasonable."

I could see the tightness gather in her face.

"She even tried to knock the fence down with her car. All she did was bash in her fender. The fence was pretty solid. One day I couldn't stand it anymore, so I put my house up for sale and bought this one. Just for spite, Victoria put hers up for sale and moved across town."

There was a pause. I cleared my throat self-consciously. Suddenly the tightness in Amanda's face relaxed and the smile returned. "Then your grandfather sought us out."

"Oh," said Carol Ann, "what did he do?"

"He was pretty tricky, he was. He came to my house and asked me if I could help him solve a problem that had been troubling him for some years. After I agreed to help, he asked me to come to his house that night for dinner. Of course, when I arrived Victoria appeared a few minutes later. He'd been to her house with the same story." Her face softened even more. "Over dinner he told us about his problem. For several years he had watched two sisters build a wall out of a fence."

Carol Ann patted my arm. "What happened then?"

"Oh, I'd like to tell you that we settled our differences then and there, but we didn't. It took some time. But without your grandfather's love for us, it never would have happened. We knew he really was troubled by our quarrel and that he really cared. A year later Victoria married again, a good man named Roy Kanell, and they moved to Fargo, North Dakota. They have four children. I've never had the opportunity to remarry." She looked at her watch. "Oh, my dears, I don't want to be rude, but I really do have to pack."

"You've been very kind," said Carol Ann.

"Could I ask one more question?" I ventured.

"Of course," replied Amanda.

"We're looking for several people who knew my grandfather. Do you happen to know anyone he might have known named Lillian?"

She stroked her chin for a moment. "I wish I could help," she said at last, "but I can't think of anyone I've ever known by that name." She retrieved our coats and led us to the front door. "Do have a Merry Christmas," she said, smiling. "And wish your dear grandmother the best from us."

"Merry Christmas to you, Amanda," said my wife. "Where will you be going?"

"To Minneapolis—St. Paul."

"Who lives there?" I asked.

"That's where you transfer to Fargo," she replied.

Chapter Twelve

The clouds were gathering again as we drove back silently to our house. The threat of snow lingered in the air. "We still have three names, William; don't get discouraged."

"Even if we never find Lillian, I'm glad we've talked to these people. I feel as if I know my grandfather better than I ever did, even though I lived with him for so many years."

"You've always said he was a private person."

"It's funny, Carol Ann, you get so used to a person's comings and goings that you don't even wonder where he's been and what he's done. I guess we just take people for granted." I opened the door for my wife and gave her a hug and a kiss.

"Grandmother," I said a few minutes later when she answered the phone, "we've just come from Amanda Grossbeck's home. She wanted us to wish you a merry Christmas."

"Is she still here?" asked my grandmother. "She's usually off to visit her sister for the holidays."

"She's leaving in the morning," I replied.

"She's such a wonderful woman. Always volunteering to help wherever she can. I've always been sorry she didn't marry again after her husband was lost in the war."

"I don't think she's ever had a chance," I replied.

"Nonsense, William, that Roy Kanell wanted to marry her but she refused, and he ended up marrying her sister. Still, it seems as if they've gotten along. Victoria was pregnant when her husband went off to war, and Roy raised the boy as if he were his own. Of course, Victoria raised his three children as if they were hers. All's well that ends well, I suppose."

"I guess I didn't know all of the story, Grandma."

"We rarely do, William."

"Well, at any rate, Amanda wanted us to wish you a merry Christmas."

"Thank you, William. See you soon."

"Good night." I hung up the phone.

My wife snuggled against me as I climbed into bed. Long after she had fallen asleep I lay awake wondering about how many people's lives my grandfather had touched. None of the things he had done seemed extra-ordinary, yet sometimes the results were profound. I drifted off to sleep.

Five golden rings, sang out the clock radio. I rubbed my eyes and groped for the shut off switch on the clock. *Four calling birds, three French hens, two . . .* I found the switch.

"Morning already?" said my wife from beneath the covers.

"Afraid so," I said groggily. "One more day until the weekend." I made my way into the bathroom and turned the water on in the shower. I let the hot water run over my head and revive me.

"Honey," called my wife. "Do you want me to try to reach Maude Carlisle today?"

"Can't hear you for the water," I called back.

She opened the bathroom door and repeated her question.

"Sure. I can get away anytime after three o'clock. The earlier the better if we're going to the high school concert tonight." I stayed under the water for a few more minutes before turning off the shower, shaving, and getting ready for work.

"See you later," I said, giving my wife a kiss good-bye. "And good luck with Mrs. Carlisle."

Last night's promise of snow had been realized, and three more inches of sparkling white had been added to the drifts in the front yard. I shoveled the driveway and moved a snowblower definitely to the top of my Christmas list. As always the town seemed wiped clean of any ugliness under the new-fallen snow. *Procrastinator,* I thought, *you'd better take some time to get your Christmas shopping done for Carol Ann.* I pulled into the agency parking lot.

Sam Adams, our custodian and all around handyman, was finishing the walks with his snow shovel. "Morning, Mr. Martin," he waved.

"Good morning, Sam," I waved back.

My secretary smiled as I entered my office. "Had to dig out again, Mr. Martin?"

I nodded my head and sat down at my desk. We were working with a number of travel agencies supplying trip cancellation insurance: Christmas always brought a flood of people taking cruises in the warm waters of the

Caribbean. Two hours later I was still working through a pile of forms when the phone rang. "It's your wife, Mr. Martin."

"Thanks." I picked up the phone. "Hello, sweetheart."

"William!" I could hear the excitement in her voice. "I've reached Maude Carlisle and she's agreed to meet us at four o'clock this afternoon. I hope you can get away in time to pick me up. She sounded really excited to see you."

"Sounds great. Where does she live? How far away?"

"About fifteen minutes. If you can pick me up at three forty-five, I'll be waiting."

"It's a date."

"William, I feel really good about this one. I think we're going to discover what we need to know."

"I hope so. Christmas is only six days away."

I was immersed the rest of the day in travel agency requests. I glanced at my watch and realized I had worked right through lunch, and it was nearly time to pick up Carol Ann.

"You've put in a hard day," said my secretary. "Will you be back this afternoon?"

"I doubt it. I've an appointment with a Mrs. Carlisle and I don't know how long it will take."

"Carlisle?" My secretary was puzzled. "I don't remember an account with that name."

"It's a personal thing," I replied. "My wife and I have an appointment . . . actually it's a pretty long, involved story. I'll see you tomorrow."

I arrived home just in time to pick up Carol Ann. She gave me the address and we started for Maude Carlisle's home. The house was located in the part of the city known as Snob Hill by most of us. The homes ranged from huge to obscene. I found it hard to believe that a woman who had done our washing and ironing would be found in such a prestigious neighborhood.

We reached the address, a large Georgian mansion flanked with six-foot-high hedges that ran down both sides of the estate. A dozen carefully trimmed pines lined both sides of a circular drive. The trees had been decorated with Christmas lights and tinsel. Between the ornate pillars, garlands of pine hung in sweeping arches. The pine boughs had been decorated with shimmering tinsel, ornaments, and lights.

We parked our car on the brick driveway that had been carefully swept of every flake of snow, and climbed the marble stairway to the front door of the mansion. Before I could reach for the brass door knocker, the door opened and a man in a cutaway coat bowed slightly in our direction. "Mr. and Mrs. Martin, I believe."

"Why, yes," I said.

"May I have your coats, please? Mrs. Carlisle is waiting in the library." He helped Carol Ann remove her coat, then took mine. "This way, please." He led us across a mosaic tile entryway toward a recessed doorway. He knocked lightly, waited a moment, then opened the door. "Mr. and Mrs. Martin, madam." He stepped back and we entered the library.

Maude Carlisle sat behind a huge rolltop desk. The walls of the library were lined with bookcases from the floor to the ten-foot-high ceiling. The windows behind Mrs. Carlisle were hung with deep blue velvet draperies tied back with gold cords. A cobalt-blue plush carpet covered the floor and absorbed any noise we might have made in walking toward the desk. To the left of the desk were a snow-white couch and love seat forming an L, with an onyx end table between them.

The Maude Carlisle I remembered had been a plump woman with dark eyes and lifeless hair. The woman who rose from behind the desk was elegant, thin and lithe. Her silver hair was arranged around her face in a way that exaggerated the size of her eyes. Only the dark eyes were the same. She was dressed in a stylish pale blue skirt and white blouse. She extended her hand to my wife. "Mrs. Martin," she purred. "And William, what a good-looking man you've grown up to be."

I blushed. "And are there any little Martins?" she asked softly.

"Not yet," I replied, unsure of what to call this person who had been our ironing lady.

"Ah, a pity," she said. "Please, have a seat." She glided across the blue carpet to the sofa, motioning toward it with her hand. We sat down slowly. Only then did she curl up on the love seat. "Now, what can I help you with?"

I stared at this elegant creature, trying to reconcile the person before me with the Maude Carlisle I had known twenty years earlier. "Mrs. Carlisle," I began.

"Oh, that's much too formal, William, for old friends. Please call me Maude."

I felt Carol Ann slide closer to me on the sofa. "Maude, then, as you probably know, my grandfather passed away last summer." I saw a hint of tears form in her eyes. She nodded. "Well, I'm trying to gather some information about him for my grandmother. We—Carol

Ann and I—have located a number of people who knew him, and we've been asking them to share their memories with us."

"Your grandmother was such a lucky woman," Maude began. "Will Martin was a true saint. And he was lucky to have found a woman like his Nell." It was obvious the tears would begin to fall at any moment.

"He *was* a good man," was all I could think of to say.

"And I believe that you, William, are much like him," she replied. "Of course, I've always felt a special kinship with you. I'm sorry we've grown so out of touch."

Carol Ann snuggled against me. "It has been a long time," I replied.

"Don't blame yourself, William; it is I who should have kept better track of you. However, with Llewelyn and me traveling so much, we've been gone more than we've been home. Time seems to slip away so fast."

"Mrs. Carlisle—Maude—I barely remember when you cleaned our house. I can't imagine why you'd feel you needed to keep track of me."

"Surely your grandparents told you what your family did for me?"

I shook my head. "Not really, Maude. That's what we're trying to do. Gather information about my grandfather." I felt an uneasy chill go down my spine. "Just exactly what did they do for you?"

Silence hung uncomfortably in the air. "William, if it weren't for your parents' accident and your grandparents' decision, I wouldn't be here."

Chapter Thirteen

Carol Ann let go of my arm and leaned forward. "What do you mean, Mrs. Carlisle?"

The color had drained from Maude's face. "Perhaps this is not the time . . ." She stood and began to pace back and forth on the carpet. "I was so anxious to see you again after all these years. But I assumed you had been told. I mean, it never entered my head that you wouldn't know."

"Know what?" asked Carol Ann.

Maude sat down heavily on the love seat. "When I was first married," she began, "Llewelyn and I were very happy. Before we married, Llewelyn had taken over a major part of his family's import and export business, much as I assume you have taken over for Will. Although he was nearly fifteen years older than I, we were very much in love. We moved into this home, the family estate. After five years of marriage, three devastating events happened in our lives. First, my father-in-law died suddenly of a heart attack. His wife had died two years before Llewelyn and I met. At his father's death, Llewelyn was plunged into inconsolable grief. He and his father had been very close. Not only did the two work together, but the three of us lived together in this house.

"Then, due to shifts in the global market, Llewelyn had to be gone for extended periods of time. The two of us had never been separated for more than a few days in five years, but now he was gone for weeks at a time. Normally I would have accompanied him, but I was diagnosed with a disease that was destroying my kidneys. I had to stay close to the hospital in order to undergo dialysis three days a week."

She shifted uncomfortably on the love seat. "The strain on Llewelyn was enormous. He'd call me every night from wherever he was to see how I was doing and bemoan the fact that his father wasn't there to help guide him at this crucial time in the business. It didn't matter that I'd assure him I was in good hands; he was more than concerned. After a several-week trip to the Far East he arrived home just before I was to go to the hospital for treatment. One of the side effects of the treatment was that I retained water. I'd added fifty pounds of weight. Llewelyn hardly recognized me. The medication I took to reduce the water retention produced a strange odor. He found that hard to stomach."

I could tell that this was a difficult recollection. Maude's face was drawn and she spoke in a monotone.

"I'm not sure how your grandfather and Llewelyn made contact, but they knew each other, of course, through the bank. Somehow I was invited to stay with your grandparents while Llewelyn traveled across the world. Your grandmother bundled me off to the hospital three times every week and made certain I took my medication. Kidney transplants were fairly new, but were promising enough that I was placed on a donor list to receive a new kidney. For the next three years I lived with your grandparents, awaiting a transplant. Llewelyn came home for a few days each month, and then was gone."

Maude arose from the love seat and began pacing the room slowly. "You knew nothing of this, William?" I shook my head. She chewed on the corner of her lip. "Do you remember much about your parents?"

"Very little, I'm afraid. I've seen their pictures, of course, and that makes me think I remember what they looked like, but I don't believe I really remember much."

"They were beautiful people, William. Your mother was an angel, and your father so much like his father." She paused and chewed on her lip again. "This might be very difficult, William. How much do you remember about their deaths?"

"I have a vague recollection of their funeral. I remember going to the cemetery in the rain. But that's about all. Why?"

"We were quite close, your parents and I. When the accident occurred they were rushed to the hospital. Your grandparents and I hurried there too. Your mother was killed instantly, but your father was still alive. Within a few moments, however, the doctors knew that he would not live. In the course of the tests it was determined that his tissue and mine were a close match. Of course, you're not supposed to know who the donor is, but these circumstances were pretty peculiar. Your grandparents had to make the decision whether to let them remove your father's kidneys and transplant them. Your grandfather wrestled with the decision for just a moment, then told them to go ahead as soon as his only son was gone."

Tears were flowing down all our cheeks as Maude sat again on the love seat. "So because your father died, I am alive. I have one of his kidneys. I have no idea where the other one went. Maybe now you understand why I feel such a kinship to you. That's why I was so delighted when your beautiful wife called. I've felt so guilty that I haven't kept better track of you."

"Thank you, Maude, for sharing that touching story with us," said my wife. "How much longer did you live with the Martins?"

"About a year. I had to be carefully watched for rejection of the new kidney, and Will and Nell looked out for me as if I were one of their own. As I began to feel better I started doing some of the housework. It was little enough to repay them."

"Where's Llewelyn?" Carol Ann asked innocently.

"Somewhere in the Mediterranean. When I turned forty-five he decided he needed a younger woman. He married a trophy wife, an eighteen-year-old he found on the French Riviera. But my lawyers were very, very good. I have the house and a substantial settlement." I detected a sadness in her voice.

"You've been so kind," I said. "I'm sure that wasn't an easy story to tell."

"I'm sure it wasn't easy to listen to," she replied. "You two hang on to each other. You're a handsome couple."

We walked out of the library into the mosaic tile hall. The manservant appeared as if by magic with our coats.

"Could I ask you one last question?" my wife asked Maude.

Maude cocked her head to one side. "Of course."

"In all the time you lived with the Martins, did you ever know anyone named Lillian?"

"Lillian? No, I don't think so. Now, Llewelyn knew a Lily in Paris, but that's as close as I can come. Why do you ask?"

"She's just one of the people we're trying to contact," replied my wife.

"Merry Christmas, Maude," I said.

"Merry Christmas to you and your good lady," she replied. The door of the mansion closed behind us.

As we sat down in the car, my wife turned to me. "Are you sorry we went there?"

"Not at all."

"Neither am I. I told you I had a good feeling about this visit."

Chapter Fourteen

That evening we attended the annual Christmas concert at the high school. The choir director and the band director apparently had overcome the artistic differences that separated them on occasion, for the music was beautiful and inspiring. As usual, a large crowd had turned out to support the concert. Afterwards, Carol Ann and I walked along arm in arm, reminiscing about past Christmases. "Well, sweetheart," I said finally, "Christmas is next Wednesday and we still haven't any idea about Lillian. What do we do now?"

"I'm not ready to give up yet. We have two more names on the list," said Carol Ann. "When you first read the list, you didn't feel very excited about the next name. Who is it?"

"Richard Leconte," I said, feeling the Christmas spirit evaporate in an instant.

"Why do you have such hard feelings about him?"

I shrugged. "I guess I don't know the whole story. Grandpa really liked Richard when he was training him at the bank, but one night Grandpa came home quite upset. Apparently Richard had done something that disturbed him. Shortly after that, Richard left and went to work for

Fairfield State Bank. I don't know that he ever spoke to Grandpa again."

"Maybe you ought to forget about seeing him," said Carol Ann.

"What?" I said, trying to appear cheerful. "And miss a chance at finding Lillian?" We walked on through the wintery night, immersed in our own thoughts.

The following Saturday dawned with lightly falling flakes as large and soft as goose down. "I've some Christmas shopping I need to finish," I said to my wife.

"So do I," she replied. "If you're going downtown today, can I drop you off at work on Monday and have the car?"

"It's a deal."

I shoveled the two inches of fluffy snow from the driveway and then made my way to the mall that had been built on the far side of town. Although it was barely nine o'clock when I arrived, there was hardly a vacant parking space. *Next year,* I thought to myself, *I am not going to procrastinate.*

The curio shop seemed less busy than the other shops, and I knew Carol Ann had been admiring the porcelain cottages they imported from Ireland. Only two other customers were carrying on a slow waltz as they moved from display to display. I found the perfect cottage, complete with thatched roof, and took it to the cash register. The girl who waited on me appeared to be no older than twelve or fourteen. She smiled broadly and tried to affect an Irish accent.

"A fine choice, sir," she said in her best brogue. Her voice hinted that she was somewhat older than she appeared. She carefully wrapped the cottage in tissue paper and then placed it in a Styrofoam box. I was reaching into my pocket for my wallet, when a customer walking past me bumped my arm.

"Sorry," he said grumpily.

"No problem," I replied as I turned to see Richard Leconte's bony figure. "Mr. Leconte," I said in surprise. "My wife and I were just talking about you last night."

His eyebrows, which looked like gray caterpillars above his dark brown eyes, rose in surprise. "Oh? You're William Martin, aren't you? And what were you saying?"

"I'm putting together some remembrances of my grandfather for my grandmother for Christmas, and I remembered that you and he had worked together. I was going to try to reach you to see if I could have a few moments of your time before Christmas."

He stared into my eyes and rubbed his chin with his hand. "Not today. I've got to finish my Christmas shopping," he said. "Would lunch on Monday suit you?"

"That would be fine," I replied. "Where would you like to meet?"

He pondered for a moment. "How about Antonio's? They serve a good pasta salad."

I nodded my head in agreement.

"Say eleven-thirty, so we beat the crowds?"

I nodded again.

"I'll see you Monday, then." He turned and strode out of the shop.

"That'll be thirty-one dollars and eighteen cents," said the wee lass behind the counter. I paid her and left.

Must be fate, I thought. *I haven't seen Richard Leconte in nearly a year. Maybe my prayers have been heard and I'm going to find Lillian.*

Shortly after noon I arrived home. I entered the kitchen and saw Carol Ann standing by the sink gazing out the window. "Now, where can I hide your presents so you won't peek?" I said mysteriously.

My wife turned around and I could see tears had been running down her cheeks. "What's the matter?" I asked.

"Call this number," she said quietly, handing me a scrap of paper.

"What's the matter?" I repeated.

"It's Alicia Blackburn. Rudy . . . oh, just call them; they'll tell you."

I dialed the number. "Williams County Social Services, how may I help you?"

"This is William Martin returning your call."

"Just one moment, Mr. Martin."

My wife had turned again to the window. "Why, when you try to do the right thing, does it always end up this way?" she asked.

Before I could reply, a familiar voice on the phone said, "Mr. Martin?"

"Yes."

"You are the only contact number we have on Alicia

Blackburn. After you called the other day we sent a social worker up to her apartment in Copper City. Apparently her husband, Rudy, was home at the time. He was quite belligerent. It appears that a fight has been going on since then. Last night he threw Alicia and the children out of the house. They were able to make their way here to Brewerton. We've put them up in a shelter for the day."

"Is she hurt? And the children?"

"They have a few bruises, but nothing serious. My reason in calling you is, as I said, you're the only contact number besides her parents. We've spoken with her mother, but her parents seem reluctant to have Alicia and her children move in with them. We're looking for any place we can put them for a month or so while we try to resolve the situation. The husband seems to have disappeared, but we have no idea when he'll return."

"Aren't there apartments there in Brewerton?" I asked.

"None that will take three children," the voice replied. "I'm calling you on the outside chance you might know of somewhere, anywhere, we could put this little family. They have so little, and it is Christmastime . . ."

A thought sprang into my head. "Let me do a little checking and I'll call you back, okay?"

"You're a lifesaver, Mr. Martin."

"I hope so," I said as I hung up the phone. I consulted the list and found Wendel Walker's number. I dialed.

"Hello," said Annie.

"Annie, this is William Martin; do you remember me?"

"Of course," she laughed. "It's my father who's forgetful, not me."

"Annie, I have a really strange request, and I'll understand if you say no, but . . ." And I explained the situation to her.

"Three children?" said Annie. "How old?"

"About six and three and a baby. Is there any chance, Annie, of their renting your apartment?" There was a pause of several seconds. *She's not going to let them in,* I thought.

"William," she said at last, "please, please bring them here."

"How much is the rent, Annie? I'm sure social services will have to know."

"Whatever they can afford, William. We'd just be honored to have them here."

"Thank you, Annie. You're an angel."

"Thank you, William, more than you know."

I hung up and called social services and let them know we'd found a place. My wife's tears had dried and she was smiling once more. "Ask them if we need to come and get them," she urged.

"Do they need a ride?" I asked the voice.

"Mr. Martin, we're over seventy-five miles away," came the astonished reply. "We can't ask you to come this far. We'll put them on a bus first thing in the morning. They can spend the night in the shelter."

"My wife and I will be there as soon as we can," I replied. "Tell me your address." I wrote it down.

"Are you sure, Mr. Martin?"

"We're sure."

Carol Ann was gathering blankets out of the linen closet. "They might be cold," she said in response to my curious look.

"Carol Ann, the car has a heater."

An hour and a half later we arrived in Brewerton. The snow continued to fall and the light was fading from the sky as we approached county social services. Alicia and her two older children were sitting quietly on a bench. The baby was asleep on a blanket next to Alicia. I could see angry welts on the children's arms. Alicia's left eye was bruised and blackened. When she saw us enter the room, tears flowed down her cheeks. Carol Ann ran to her, pulled her to her feet, and hugged her. The little girl threw her arms around her little brother protectively and pulled him close to her.

"Mr. Martin?" said an ample woman sitting behind a table across the room. I nodded. "Thank you for coming. Did you find out how much the rent will be?" She poised her pencil above a form on the table.

"Whatever you can afford . . . whatever the standard rate is."

The woman's eyebrow raised. "That's a little unusual, Mr. Martin."

"Well, these are unusual people," I replied. I explained the situation with Wendel Walker and his daughter.

She shrugged her shoulders and wrote a figure on the form. "Please sign here," she said, turning the form in my direction.

I scanned down the form. "We're really not trying to assume custody of these people," I said.

"Just a formality," said the woman. "We'll need to do an assessment before permanent arrangements are made. But I can't release her until I know someone will look out for her welfare." I signed.

My wife and Alicia were still hugging and sobbing. I walked over to the little girl and boy, who were still tightly entwined. "My name's William," I said, kneeling in front of them. "What's yours?"

The little girl set her mouth in a straight line and stared defiantly at me. The little boy closed his eyes.

"It's all right, Ruth; they're friends," said Alicia through her tears.

"You told us not to talk to strangers," replied the little girl.

"They're not strangers, Ruth," said Alicia quietly. She turned to me. "William, this is my daughter, Ruth, and my son Randy, and the baby is Little Rudy."

The six of us piled into the car and started the drive back to Alicia's new apartment. The snow settled softly on the ground.

Chapter Fifteen

Sunday morning dawned cold and clear. The snow squeaked underfoot as we walked to church. "Annie seemed genuinely excited to have Alicia and her brood there," I said.

My wife nodded. "So did her father. From your description, I thought he just sat in his rocking chair and slept. He was smiling and holding the little boy on his knee. I think they've brought some life into the house."

"What did you think of the apartment?" I asked.

"I'm sure it's several steps up from what they're used to. It seems a little bare, though, without a Christmas tree."

"My thoughts exactly," I said. "Maybe tomorrow night we can do something about that."

Carol Ann squeezed my arm. "I was going to suggest they join us for dinner today, but Annie was too fast for me. It's probably better that they have a little time to settle in anyway," she said.

The rest of the day went by quietly. After dinner I banished Carol Ann from our bedroom and wrapped the gifts I had bought for her. I carried them into my study and hid them in a closet.

"William," said my wife as we lay in bed that night, "I'm going to drop over to Alicia's tomorrow and find out what their clothing sizes are."

"While you're there, ask her if she knows Lillian," I said as I pulled the quilt up to ward off the winter chill.

At eleven-fifteen the next day I wrapped my overcoat around me and began the four-block walk from the agency to Antonio's restaurant. Last-minute shoppers were scurrying around the city.

Five minutes after I arrived, Richard Leconte burst through the door. His eyes adjusted to the darker interior and he spotted me sitting at a table in one corner. He crossed the restaurant swiftly and sat down. A waiter appeared almost immediately, and we gave him our orders.

"Are you having a busy day?" Richard asked.

"Not much going on in the insurance world," I replied. "How's the banking business?"

"Brisk," he replied. "I've got to get back as soon as I can. So if you don't mind, let's get right to what you want."

"I'm just gathering some information on my grandfather," I began.

"William Martin was the most honest man I've ever known," he interrupted. "I've been thinking about him ever since you and I met last Saturday. I've wondered what you'd like to know."

I was quite surprised by this response, since I'd been

led to believe that Richard and my grandfather had a strong dislike for each other. "Well, anything you'd like to tell me. Although I do have one specific question I'd like you to answer if you can."

He seemed not to pay any attention to what I had said. "I have often wished I had never made the stupid mistakes I did that led to our parting of the ways." He looked into my face with his deep brown eyes, trying to see if I understood what he was saying.

"I know very little of what went on between the two of you," I said at last.

"Maybe it's better left forgotten and unsaid," he mused. "But then, maybe you can learn from the mistake of a stupid old man." He gazed around the room. His eyes seemed to lose focus, as if he were looking into the past. "The bank only had two offices when your grandfather and I first worked there. We knew every customer by name, and I think Will knew everyone's balance by heart. He taught me everything he knew about the banking business. We were the closest of friends. Until . . ."

The waiter brought our food and placed it on the table. "Thank you," I said.

"Will had been looking at banks in other communities and realized we needed to expand. The world was changing, and people wanted the convenience of banking close to home. He took me aside and asked if I would support him with the board of directors. He wanted to open a small branch where the shopping mall was being built." He paused and forked a mouthful of pasta into his mouth.

"That seems like a smart decision to me," I replied.

Richard swallowed his food. "From this perspective it makes perfect sense, but not forty years ago. Banks were big, stable buildings in the middle of town. They just weren't building little branches spread out from the center of town. There was worry about them being easy to rob. We worried about the increased cost of operating multiple offices. It just wasn't a popular decision. But Will asked for my support, and I told him I'd follow him to the end of the earth." He paused and took another bite of food.

"Then what happened?" I asked.

The corners of his mouth tugged down and he pursed his lips. "Then we had a meeting with the board of directors. The chairman of the board lived down the street from me. We went to the same church. He and my father were classmates in college. Our families went back a long way together. Anyway, Will presented his proposal to open a branch in the mall, and he turned to me for support. The chairman looked me straight in the eye and said, 'Richard, you can't support this fool idea, can you?'"

He twirled the pasta on his plate with his fork. "So there I was, caught between the proverbial rock and a hard place. I'd promised Will my support, but it was clear the chairman wanted me to back him. I hemmed and hawed a little, then sided with the chairman. I had a wife and children to support, don't you see—I couldn't risk losing my job. At least, that's how I've justified my action."

"I understand," I said, wondering how I'd behave in a similar situation.

"But your grandfather just wouldn't give up. He tried a second time to explain the benefits of opening that branch. He made a lot of sense, but the chairman just wouldn't buy it. He asked me again, 'Richard, you can't believe this will work, can you?' And again I agreed that the chairman was right."

"How did my grandfather react?" I asked.

"He looked across the table at me with those puppy dog eyes of his and pleaded for my support. He made one last attempt to sell his idea, with the same results. After the meeting I tried to explain my position, but I think he was too hurt to listen."

"Then what happened?"

Richard Leconte gazed across the restaurant and out the front window at the people scurrying by. "Then, of course, your grandfather was proven right. Another bank began building a branch at the mall site, and several others sprang up around town. Our bank began to lose customers and had to cut back. My position was eliminated and I went to work for Fairfield State Bank. Will was promoted and in time built the bank into one of the largest in the state by opening branch offices where people wanted them."

"It seems like an honest mistake to me. I can see your point of view," I replied.

"My boy, you don't understand. Once you give your word to someone, never go back on it. Once you do, it's hard to live with yourself. If I had stood by your grandfather, we both would have prospered with the bank. Even though your grandfather forgave me, perhaps I wouldn't have carried this guilt. And I could have looked him in the eye, which I never could do until the day he died," he finished in a whisper.

"But enough about the musings of an old man, what is it you wanted me to answer?"

I cleared my throat. "I'm trying to find a number of my grandfather's acquaintances. Did you ever know a woman by the name of Lillian?"

"Lillian who?" he asked.

"I don't know her last name, I'm afraid. I was hoping you might be able to help," I replied.

Richard Leconte stared at the tabletop in front of him. Then he shook his head slowly. "I wish I could help you, my boy, but I'm afraid I can't. I'd do anything to help Will Martin."

The waiter appeared with our check. "I'll get it," said Richard. "It's the least I can do." We rose from the table. "And, William, good luck with your quest."

I shook his hand. "Thank you, Richard," I smiled. We walked out of the restaurant side by side.

Chapter Sixteen

At four-thirty my wife picked me up at the agency. "Any luck with Mr. Leconte?" she asked.

"No," I said, "at least no luck with Lillian. But I don't think he and my grandfather were quite as competitive as I'd been led to believe."

"Well, we still have the Yazzie woman," she replied with a smile on her face.

"Did you have a busy day?" I asked.

Carol Ann nodded her head. "Your shopping is finished and I have sizes for the Blackburns. How about catching dinner downtown and doing a little more shopping?"

"How's the budget holding up?" I asked.

Carol Ann avoided my eyes for a moment; then she said, "Will you really be disappointed if you don't get a snowblower for Christmas? I spent quite a bit of money on the Blackburns, and I still have a long list to complete."

I laughed. "I need the exercise anyway."

We stopped at our favorite Mexican restaurant and ate the Rio Grande Special, which was enough food for four people. Completely stuffed, we began shopping for children's clothing and toys. We arrived home just before ten o'clock. Carol Ann had placed my gifts beneath the Christmas tree. I retrieved hers and placed them there as well. "We're an awfully lucky couple, aren't we?" I said.

It was nearly midnight before we finished wrapping the gifts for the Blackburns. "Tomorrow is Christmas Eve, a perfect time to deliver," said my wife.

Lillian, I thought as I drifted off to sleep that night. *Who is Lillian?*

I awoke the next morning to the odor of frying bacon. I glanced at the clock radio. I had forgotten to turn it on the night before, and I had only thirty minutes to get to the office. I jumped out of bed and rushed through a shower. Carol Ann had the plates on the table as I hurried into the kitchen.

"Hurry up, sleepyhead," she said as I wolfed down the food.

Still swallowing my last bite of toast, I kissed her quickly and ran out the door. "See you this afternoon," I called over my shoulder. "We have our annual office party at lunch, and then I'll be home about one-thirty."

"Shall I try to get hold of Mrs. Yazzie?"

"Sure. Anytime after one-thirty." I backed out of the garage and drove to the office. I was only five minutes late.

The caterer showed up around eleven o'clock and began setting food out on a table in the boardroom. Work essentially came to a halt. We ate and wished each other good cheer. I handed out Christmas bonuses. We had had a good year, and the amounts were substantial. By one o'clock the last piece of ham and turkey had disappeared and our agents were headed out the door. I paid the caterer and helped him get the trays back into his van. At one-thirty I pulled into our garage.

"We have a two-thirty appointment with Beatrice Yazzie," said my wife as I walked through the door. "But we'll have to go to the hospital to see her."

"Is she seriously ill?" I asked.

"No," my wife chuckled, "she works there and her shift goes until eleven o'clock tonight. So I thought it better if we went there. She didn't seem to mind."

"That gives us an hour to deliver our gifts to the Blackburns," I said. We loaded the presents into the car and headed toward Wendel Walker's home. As we pulled up in front of the house, I noticed that the *"Apartment for Rent"* sign was missing from the window. We gathered as many presents as we could carry and made our way up the front porch. As I struggled to reach the doorbell, the door flew open and Annie stood there.

"What have you two been up to?" she chortled.

"Just a few things for the Blackburns," replied Carol Ann.

"Come in, come in," she said. "Just put them under the Christmas tree in the living room. We're all going to celebrate together in the morning."

We entered the living room and saw Wendel Walker sitting in his rocking chair. A smile creased his face as we entered. "Annie," he wheezed, "are we going to have more company for Christmas?"

"This is William Martin and his sweet wife," she replied. "He came to see you the other day, Daddy."

Wendel began rocking his chair vigorously. "It's going to be a great Christmas," he said. "Just like old times."

There were a number of packages under the tree as we went to place ours there. "You're not the only ones who can go shopping," smiled Annie.

We carried the rest of the gifts into the house and realized we had not seen any of the Blackburns. "Is Alicia doing all right?" asked my wife.

Tears filled Annie's eyes. "Oh, right now she's still blaming herself for what happened. It will take a while until she realizes her husband is at least equal in the blame. She's kind of hiding from you, I think, because you saw her when she was most vulnerable. It will take a little while yet before she's comfortable. But," she said brightly, "it's going to be a great Christmas in this house."

I shook Wendel's translucent paw and gave Annie a hug as we left their home. As I let my wife into the car I spotted a little girl at a downstairs window. She waved slowly to me. I waved back.

We drove to the hospital and arrived just before two-thirty. The automatic doors swished open. We approached the information desk. "Could you tell us where we could find Beatrice Yazzie?" I asked.

The woman behind the desk pecked away at the computer. "I'm sorry," she said, "we don't have anyone here by that name."

"Are you sure?" I said. "We had an appointment with her at two-thirty."

"Spell the last name for me," said the woman.

"Y-A-Z-Z-I-E," I replied.

Her fingers pecked again at the keyboard. She shook her head. "Sorry, we don't have any patients by that name."

"Oh," said my wife, "she's not a patient; she works here."

"Why didn't you say so?" the woman snapped. She entered the name in the computer. "Go down this hall to the first hallway on the right and then just keep going to the end," she directed.

"Where are we headed?" asked Carol Ann.

"The blood bank," came the reply.

Chapter Seventeen

We followed the instructions to the blood bank. The doors opened to a small reception area. Another woman sat behind a desk. "Fill out this card, please," she said, holding out a card to each of us.

"We didn't come to donate blood," I said.

"Oh, well, test results aren't ready until after four o'clock."

"I'm sorry," I said, "we have an appointment with Beatrice Yazzie. Could you tell us where we can find her?"

"She's in the donor room," she said, jerking her thumb over her shoulder toward some double doors behind her.

"Is it all right if we go in?"

"Sure. Maybe you'll change your minds and give us a pint," she cackled.

We walked through the doors into the donor room. There were six cots lined up in two rows of three. Only two cots were filled. A tall blond woman in a nurse's uniform was attending to the donors. A short, black-haired woman sat at a desk in the corner filling out forms. The sounds of Christmas carols played softly in the background. A plastic bag hung at the side of each cot. One was nearly filled with dark red blood; the other was just beginning to fill. The blond woman snapped her finger against the plastic tubing attached to one bag.

We walked to the woman at the desk. "We're here to see Mrs. Yazzie," said my wife.

"Over there," said the black-haired woman, pointing to the tall blond.

Beatrice heard her name and looked back over her shoulder. "You must be the Martins," she said. "Have a seat and I'll be with you in a minute." She stripped the blood from the transparent tube, clipped it off, and rotated the bag a few times. She then pulled the needle from the donor's arm, placed a cotton ball over the wound, and taped it in place.

"You've done this before, honey, haven't you?" The donor nodded his head. "Just lie here quietly for a minute; then when you feel okay, ask Florence to help you get some juice and a cookie. And merry Christmas."

She jiggled the other bag, then came over to where we were sitting. "So you're Will Martin's grandson. You look just like him . . . well, a little younger perhaps."

I stood and shook her hand. "This is my wife, Carol Ann. She's the one who called you today."

Beatrice shook hands with Carol Ann and sat down beside us. "What can I do for you?"

I began the now familiar explanation of what we were trying to do for my grandmother. "I'm wondering why your name appeared in my grandfather's journal," I concluded.

Beatrice's eyes wandered over to the wall above

Florence's head. "Do you see those gold drops of blood over there?"

We looked at perhaps thirty plastic drops that were hanging on the wall. Each was about three inches long and had something written on it. "Go take a look," suggested Beatrice.

Carol Ann and I walked across the room and looked at the golden drops. Above them was a small plaque that read, "*One Golden Drop Equals a Gallon.*" Beatrice was right behind us. "When you've donated eight pints of blood, we put your name on one of these golden drops and hang it on the wall."

I moved a little closer. The first drop had the name Will Martin written on it. So did the second, and the third. I began to count. Twenty of the thirty drops had my grandfather's name written on them.

"Your grandfather was a regular. He donated four times a year for nearly forty years. When he turned sixty-five, we only had him come in when we desperately needed his blood type. He was AB negative, you know, the rarest kind."

"I had no idea," I said. "He never mentioned this at home that I can remember."

"It doesn't take that long, only about thirty minutes. He used to come during lunch. That was when I worked the day shift."

"I'm amazed," said Carol Ann.

"He was one of a kind," said Beatrice Yazzie. "I hated to see him go."

"So did we," I said wholeheartedly.

"But at least he got his wish," she said.

"What do you mean?" asked my wife.

"He went quickly. He used to tell me that after all the hours he'd spent visiting the sick in the nursing home, he knew there were things that were a lot worse than death. He used to say, 'Beatrice, if I've earned any gift from God, it's that I just want to go quickly.' And he got his wish."

She pointed toward the chairs. "Please have a seat; I need to check on a donor." She walked to where the last donor was lying on her cot. Florence had helped the other donor to a cup of juice and a cookie.

"What exactly did you want to know about your grandfather?" Beatrice asked when she returned.

"You've told us something about him that we knew nothing about, just another piece of a complex and private man. But we're also trying to locate another person who knows more about my grandfather. Do you by chance know anyone named Lillian that he might have known?"

"Get that, will you Florence?" She indicated the donor bag that was nearly full, then turned back to me. "Lillian, hmm. Do you know her last name?"

I shook my head. "That's been one of our frustrations."

"I'm sorry, I don't know anyone by that name. Anything else?"

"I don't wish to pry," said Carol Ann, "but isn't Yazzie a Navajo name?"

Beatrice smiled. "Sure is. I met Sam Yazzie when we were both students at Arizona State University. My maiden name is Jorgenson. Does that make more sense?"

She laughed. "You're not the first ones to be surprised."

I held out my hand. "Thank you for your time," I said. "And merry Christmas."

"What blood type are you, William? We're always looking for more golden drops."

"I don't know," I admitted.

"Please come back," she said with a smile. "People need you."

"I promise I will," I said.

Carol Ann and I walked out of the double doors of the donor room and into the corridor that led from the hospital. "That does it," I said. "Our last name, the last lead to Lillian. I've failed, Carol Ann."

"Oh, William," she said, "it's only four o'clock on Christmas Eve; we haven't failed yet."

We walked slowly to our car. I let my wife in and walked around the car. I slid onto the seat and closed the door. "Where do we turn?" I asked myself out loud.

"I wonder," said Carol Ann, "which nursing home he visited."

Chapter Eighteen

We rushed back into the hospital as quickly as we could and found Beatrice Yazzie. "Do you have any idea which nursing home my grandfather visited?" I asked.

"Probably the old Martha Fields Home, just down the street. It's a home for people who are terminally ill. Just go down Grove to Fifth and turn right. It's the second building on the left."

"Merry Christmas," we called out in unison as we scampered back to the car.

We drove quickly to the location. The Martha Fields Home was an old mansion that had been converted to a life-care facility. We walked up the sandstone steps and onto the porch. I rang the bell and a cheery voice called from inside, "Come in."

We entered a long hall that led to a desk with a shaded lamp on it. A white-clothed attendant sat behind the desk. She stood as we approached. "Can I help you?"

"I certainly hope so. My name is William Martin and this is my wife, Carol Ann."

Before I could go any further the attendant said, "Oh, we wondered if you'd be coming this year. Let me get Mr.

Crawford." She turned and walked through a doorway behind her.

"It sounds as if we were expected," puzzled Carol Ann. "I wonder why."

Mr. Crawford appeared. He was a man in his early fifties dressed in black slacks and a gray turtleneck. Horn-rimmed glasses were perched on his hawklike nose. He ran one hand through his thick gray hair as if trying to comb it into place, and he stuck out the other toward me. "Mr. Martin, how good of you to come. And this must be Mrs. Martin. How delightful. Your grandfather spoke so highly of you. And you look so much like him."

"Thank you," I managed to say.

"We wondered if the tradition would continue, with your grandfather's untimely passing and all. What a delight to see you."

"Tradition?" I said.

"The Christmas gifts for our patients. That is why you've come, isn't it?" He appeared a bit embarrassed.

My wife pinched me. "Of course, Mr. Crawford," I said. "We're sorry we're so late."

"Not at all, not at all," he beamed.

"We were just a little unsure of the arrangements," chipped in my wife.

"Well, do you want to continue the way your grand-father did in the past?"

"I suppose so," I said. "Could you explain it to us? He didn't leave much in the way of instructions."

"Generally he just gave us a donation and we shopped for our patients. Although one year he did the shopping himself. But I think he realized we knew more of what they needed than he did, so most years we did the shopping."

"How much money does it take?" I asked a little fearfully.

"Oh, last year we spent nearly a hundred dollars," he said, wrinkling his brow. "But we realize that may be an exorbitant amount."

"Just a hundred dollars?" I said. "How many patients do you have?"

"Only twelve. Twelve who require round-the-clock care, I'm afraid."

"How long do they usually stay?" inquired my wife.

Mr. Crawford looked a bit uncomfortable. "That's hard to say. Most of them live out the last few weeks of their lives with us. A few stay somewhat longer. Two of those we have here were here last year," he said brightening up a bit.

Carol Ann whispered in my ear, "Here goes the rest of your snowblower." She opened her purse, removed five twenty-dollar bills, and handed the cash to Mr. Crawford. "Please, take this," she said. "We wouldn't want the tradition to die."

He practically beamed from head to toe. "Would you like to visit any of the patients?" he asked. "They seem to enjoy visitors, although most of them aren't too alert, poor dears." He indicated a hallway behind him. "Six are on this floor and six are upstairs."

Carol Ann took my arm and we followed Mr. Crawford. He pushed open a door into a well-furnished bedroom. A frail, white-haired man lay on the bed. "Charlie," Mr. Crawford called out. "You have visitors."

The old man's eyelids flickered open and he rolled his head to look in our direction. "These are the Martins. I don't think you met their grandfather." Crawford turned and whispered to us, "Charlie's only been here since October. He has pancreatic cancer and probably only has a few more days."

I reached out and patted Charlie's hand. He looked at me with eyes that were dark pools of pain. "Merry Christmas, Charlie," I said.

We moved quietly into the hallway. "This must be awfully tough on you, Mr. Crawford," said my wife. "You must get attached to these people and then you see all of them pass away."

"I'd like to say you get used to it, but you don't," he said. "But I look at it this way: Charlie's in pain. When we control it with medication, he can barely open his eyes. What's worse—going on like that, or death? So we rejoice for them when they go."

We had passed a room on our journey. "Empty room?" said my wife.

"Oh, no. I wish it were. She's been here for twenty-two years, and she spent two years in a hospital before they transferred her here. She's been in a coma for all that time. And in all those years the only person who ever visited her was your grandfather."

"What happened to her?" I asked.

"She fell asleep at the wheel and crashed into another car. Two people were killed and Lillian's been in a coma ever since."

"Twenty-four years ago?" I said. He nodded his head.

"May we see her?" my wife asked quietly.

"Of course." Mr. Crawford opened the door.

In contrast to Charlie's room, Lillian's was stark white and completely devoid of any decoration. She lay in bed, her shriveled mouth open and her sightless eyes staring straight ahead. Her snow-white hair was combed straight down to her shoulders. Her clawlike fingers were partially closed, as if she were grasping a stick. She breathed a slow, rhythmic beat. An intravenous tube was attached to the back of her right hand.

"Lillian," Mr. Crawford said in a kind voice, "your old friend Will's grandson and granddaughter are here to see you." There was no flicker of recognition. "She's always the same," Mr. Crawford told us.

"Does she have any family?" asked Carol Ann.

"Oh, yes, a family of record, but they've never been here to see her. I've been here nearly twenty-five years and I can assure you that the only visitor Lillian has ever had was your grandfather."

We stayed a few more minutes, then told Mr. Crawford we had to go.

"Come back anytime. I'll introduce you to our other patients. And thank you so much for continuing the tradition." He patted his pocket where he'd placed the hundred dollars. "I'll get out immediately and pick up a few things for these good people." He waved good-bye.

We walked slowly down the sandstone steps to the car. "We found her, William, we found her," said Carol Ann solemnly.

"Twenty-four years," I repeated. "When I was four years old."

Chapter Nineteen

A brisk breeze was blowing the snow across the road as Carol Ann and I awoke on Christmas morning. We turned on the Christmas tree lights and started a fire in the fireplace, then knelt in front of the couch and thanked God for his goodness in blessing us with all we had. I turned to the second chapter of St. Luke and read the real Christmas story: "And it came to pass in those days, that there went out a decree from Caesar Augustus, that all the world should be taxed. . . . And Joseph also went up from Galilee, out of the city of Nazareth, into Judaea, unto the city of David, which is called Bethlehem . . . to be taxed with Mary his espoused wife, being great with child . . ."

Carol Ann was thrilled with her ceramic cottage. I was delighted with new insulated gloves.

"There's no snowblower under the tree," Carol Ann said.

"Maybe next year," I replied.

"Maybe," she said. "Don't you think we'd better visit your grandmother?"

"Why don't we drop by Wendel Walker's home on the way," I suggested.

We dressed and drove to the Walker home. I worried

that we were too early. It was barely eight o'clock. However, as we climbed the front steps we could hear noise from inside. I rang the bell.

"Merry Christmas," exclaimed Annie's voice as she opened the door for us.

"Are we too early?"

"Early? We've been up for hours, my boy. Come in."

Wrapping paper was strewn all over the living room. Alicia sat on the couch wearing the new clothes Carol Ann had picked out for her. Wendel sat in his rocking chair grinning from ear to ear. "Welcome. Merry Christmas," he called out.

The children were playing with their toys. "You've made this the grandest Christmas we've had in years," said Annie. "How did you know we were so lonely and needed such lively company?" I shrugged my shoulders.

Carol Ann sat down next to Alicia. "Thank you, Alicia."

"For what?" she said in amazement.

"For letting us into your life." The two of them wept together.

"Time for breakfast," called out Annie. We all trooped into the kitchen and filled our plates with ham and eggs and pancakes.

"Try some of this grape juice," she said. "It's Juliano's."

Finally filled to the brim, we said our good-byes and left for Grandmother's house. "What will become of Rudy and Alicia, I wonder," said my wife.

"Hard to say. I guess only time will tell. But somehow I think things are going to work out for the best."

We pulled up in front of my grandmother's house. As

we approached the front door she threw it open and called out, "Merry Christmas. You're just in time for breakfast."

Regardless of our protests, she made us eat another plate of food. Then we sat down in the living room. Grandmother's Christmas tree gave off a heavenly aroma. She reached beneath the tree and handed Carol Ann a small wrapped package. "Open it," she smiled.

Carol Ann unwrapped a companion cottage to the one I had given her. "How did you know?" she asked.

"I have friends in high places," she answered. She handed me an even smaller package. I opened it and found a small key inside.

"I don't understand . . ."

"It's to the snowblower in the garage," she said, smiling. "But do an old lady a favor and clean my walks off too."

"I will; you can be sure of that."

"Grandmother, you'll have to come with us to get your present," said Carol Ann.

"Where are we going?" she asked cautiously.

"Just put on your coat," said my wife.

The three of us drove to the nursing home. Mr. Crawford greeted us as we entered. "It's so good to see the two of you again. And who might this be?"

"This is my grandmother, Nell Martin."

"I'm honored, Mrs. Martin." He bowed, then turned toward Carol Ann and me, "Would you like to see what we've done with your gift?"

"In a minute, Mr. Crawford, but first we need to introduce my grandmother to one of your patients."

He nodded and we led Grandmother down the hall to Lillian's room. The door opened silently. The room was as we had left it the night before except for a large red poinsettia on the table at the foot of the bed.

"Grandmother," I said, "meet Lillian. Lillian, this is Will Martin's wife."

She studied Lillian for a moment and then a flicker of recognition crossed my grandmother's face. "Oh, William," she whispered softly.

I nodded my head. My grandmother reached down and took the withered claw of a hand in hers and gently stroked the snow-white hair. Lillian gazed straight ahead at the poinsettia.

"Thank you, William," said my grandmother. "Merry Christmas."

"Merry Christmas, Grandmother. Merry Christmas, Lillian."

From somewhere in the nursing home came the strains of *Silent night, holy night.*

Carol Ann squeezed my arm. "Merry Christmas, sweetheart."

About the Author

Richard M. Siddoway was raised in Salt Lake City, Utah. He received his bachelor's degree from the University of Utah and his master's degree in instructional systems and learning resources from the same institution. A professional educator for over thirty years, he is currently the director of the Electronic High School for the State of Utah and was recently elected to represent his district in the Utah State Legislature. He is a former bishop and now serves as stake president of the Val Verda Stake in Bountiful, Utah. In addition to *The Christmas Wish*, he is the author of the best-selling book *Twelve Tales of Christmas, Mom—and Other Great Women I've Known,* and *Habits of the Heart.*

The author and his wife, the former Geri Hendrickson, had six children prior to her untimely death from cancer. He has since married the former Janice Spires, and they have a combined family of eight children.